ZaCK
STRIKEs BaCK

Other "Saved by the Bell" titles include:

Mark-Paul Gosselaar: Ultimate Gold

Mario Lopez: High-Voltage Star

Behind the Scenes at "Saved by the Bell"

Beauty and Fitness with "Saved by the Bell"

Bayside Madness

California Scheming

ZaCK STRiKES BaCK

by Beth Cruise

Collier Books
Macmillan Publishing Company
New York
Maxwell Macmillan Canada
Toronto
Maxwell Macmillan International
New York   Oxford   Singapore   Sydney

Collier Books
Macmillan Publishing Company
866 Third Avenue
New York, NY 10022

Maxwell Macmillan Canada, Inc.
1200 Eglinton Avenue East
Suite 200
Don Mills, Ontario M3C 3N1

Macmillan Publishing Company is part of the Maxwell
Communication Group of Companies.

First Collier Books edition 1992
Printed in the United States of America
10 9 8 7 6 5 4 3 2

Library of Congress Cataloging-in-Publication Data
Cruise, Beth.
Zack strikes back / by Beth Cruise. — 1st Collier Books ed.
p.   cm.
Summary: The "Saved by the Bell" gang suffers from the mid-
semester blues, until a prankster strikes at Bayside High.
ISBN 0-02-042777-8
[1. Practical jokes—Fiction. 2. Schools—Fiction.] I. Title.
PZ7.C88827Zad   1992
[Fic]—dc20   92-5182

To Peter Engel

ZaCK
STRiKEs BaCK

Chapter 1

Zack Morris strolled down the sidewalk on his way to the Max, the Bayside High hangout. Passing a window, he smoothed his blond hair and practiced his killer grin. Still smiling to himself, he pulled open the door of the Max. Just as he headed inside, he caught sight of a pack of runners on their way up the street, and the smile quickly faded.

"They're coming!" someone shouted, pointing excitedly. "The runners! Great," Zack moaned. "This is just what I need."

"Oh, my gosh!" Kelly Kapowski exclaimed, her long, dark hair flying. "I told Cody I'd cheer him on." She pushed good-looking A. C. Slater, captain of the football and wrestling teams, out of the booth, then hopped over his legs to run toward the door. Kelly had been going steady with the school hunk, Cody Durant, for a couple of months now. He was running in the Sidewalks-to-Sand Minimarathon.

The fifteen-mile race started at city hall in downtown Palisades and wound through different neighborhoods all the way to the beach. Zack had considered it, since he was on the track team, but there was no way he'd huff and puff alongside Cody, the golden surfer god, as he breezed his way to the finish line.

Slater trailed after Kelly as a big group of kids crowded on the sidewalk and watched as the first runners approached.

Zack got a sinking feeling in his stomach when he saw that Cody Durant led the pack. The hunk's bronzed chest was bare, and his muscular legs pumped as he ran easily. His black hair was held back from his forehead by a violet bandanna. When he caught sight of the cheering Kelly, he flashed a wide grin.

"He's not so hot," Zack muttered as Samuel Powers, better known as Screech, appeared on the scene. Screech was a tall, skinny dynamo who looked as if he'd been stretched a few inches and then put into a light socket.

Screech nodded vigorously, agreeing with Zack. "Not if you don't like exceptionally handsome guys," he said.

Disgusted, Zack watched as Kelly held up a plastic bottle filled with water. Cody paused just long enough to take it from her hand in a sweeping motion. He dunked the water over his head and then tossed it away. Now his muscles glistened as well as gleamed. Suddenly, Zack *did* feel sick.

Kelly turned away dreamily as everyone headed back into the Max. "Isn't he wonderful?" she sighed. "I've never been so happy in my life."

Zack slid into the gang's regular booth, a tragic look in his hazel eyes. Cody was all Kelly ever talked about. Just because the guy was gorgeous, had an incredible body, and was devoted to Kelly, was that any reason for her to adore him?

It was all my fault, Zack thought glumly. He'd been the one who had let Kelly go junior year. He'd been in love with her for years, but when they'd finally gone steady, things just didn't work out. When Kelly had told him that they should break up, he hadn't fought for her—he'd just agreed. He'd thought that he'd be free to chase all those girls who had tantalized him while he was with Kelly. But now that he was free to date again, he only wanted to date Kelly.

Just then Lisa Turtle approached the table. Lisa was a pretty black teen whose wardrobe was top priority. Or was it boys? It changed from one day to the next. But today she was looking glum.

"What's the matter, Lisa?" Kelly asked, concerned. Lisa sighed as she slid into the booth. "I don't know," she said. "Life is just so *dull*."

Slater shook his curly dark hair. "It's the midterm blues," he said. "Nothing can shake 'em." He sunk down farther in his seat, his muscular arms crossed.

Lisa's soft brown eyes were mournful. "Even the thought of shopping doesn't excite me."

"Oh, no!" Jessie Spano exclaimed as she came up to the booth. "Things must be really terrible." Jessie was Slater's girlfriend, even though they seemed to argue more than anything else. She had a great mind *and* a great body, but the first was more important.

"Does the thought of *me* excite you, Lisa?" Screech asked. Screech had had a crush on Lisa since grade school.

"Well," Lisa said, "I admit that I'm tempted."

Practically swooning, Screech batted his eyelashes at her. "You are?"

"You bet," Lisa said. "I'm tempted to buy you a one-way ticket to Bora Bora."

Screech put a hand to his heart. "You *do* care," he said. "I just love the South Pacific."

"I'd be glad to be anywhere but here," Zack grumbled.

Kelly Kapowski shook her head. Her tanned skin glowed against the white tank top she wore. "I don't know what's wrong with you guys," she complained happily, her deep blue eyes sparkling. "I think things are terrific."

"Hey," Jessie said. "Did you guys see the race? Cody was in the lead. He looked great."

"He sure is gorgeous," Lisa cooed, brightening up a little.

"Down, girls," Zack said dryly. "Cody really isn't that exciting."

The girls all gave Zack a give-me-a-break look.

Frowning, Slater leaned toward Jessie and tapped her on the arm. "Whoa, babe," he said. "If you want to see some muscles, you don't have to look very far." Slater worked out almost every day, and he had the body to prove his devotion to sports.

"You're right, Slater," Jessie declared. "I just saw lots of muscles on the street when the guys ran by. It wasn't far to look at all." Her light hazel eyes sparkled at him mischievously. Everyone knew that she was teasing. Jessie was crazy about Slater, and the feeling was mutual.

Kelly sighed. "Cody is just so sweet. He wore my bandanna in the race for luck."

The sound of jangling bells suddenly interrupted their conversation. A hand gripped the edge of the seat behind Kelly's head. The arm was covered in silver bracelets, some of which were fashioned with little bells. A small face rose up from the booth next to them. It was a woman. Her eyes were lined with kohl, and she wore a spangled scarf around her head.

"There is no luck, young lady," she told Kelly in a heavily accented voice. "There is only fate."

Everyone stared at the woman in astonishment. The booth next to them had been empty a moment before. And the woman was completely different from anyone you normally saw in Palisades. She didn't have blond hair, she wasn't wearing a T-shirt, and she wasn't the least bit tan.

"Who are you?" Lisa asked.

"I am Rosina," the woman said, inclining her head. "I have come from the mountains and the mists of my country. I saw a new land in a vision, with blue sky and blue water. And I knew I must come over the sea." She fixed each of them in turn with her dark, compelling eyes. "I have much to learn, but I came to teach also. About fate, destiny—forces beyond our knowing. Here in America you do not respect fate."

"Do you tell fortunes?" Lisa asked breathlessly.

"I tell what can be," Rosina said with a shrug. "I do have this gift."

"You mean you can read our palms?" Jessie asked eagerly.

Rosina shook her head. "Your feet."

Zack and Slater snickered, but when Rosina looked at them, they stopped laughing. There was something about her glittering gaze that was decidedly spooky.

"The soles of the feet hold more secrets than the palms of the hands," she said. "Scoff if you will, but it is so."

"Gosh, it's so . . . mysterious," Lisa said.

"Mystical," Jessie agreed.

"Far out," Screech breathed.

"Five bucks," Rosina said.

Lisa dug into her pink patent leather purse. "I'm first," she declared. She handed five dollars over the seat to Rosina.

"Come this way," Rosina said. "We'll use a booth in the back for privacy." She rose, gathered up her long skirt in her hand, and moved toward the booth by the kitchen.

"Wish me luck," Lisa said with a giggle. She slipped out of the booth and ran toward the back.

"Zere ees no luck," Zack said, imitating Rosina's accent. "Zere ees on-lee fate."

"Zere ees also onion rings," Slater said, moving the plate toward him. "And I'd rather swallow them than mumbo jumbo." He popped one in his mouth.

"I think we should give Rosina a chance," Jessie argued. "Don't you believe in psychics, Slater?"

"Sure I do," Slater said. "As a matter of fact, I've been told that *I'm* psychic."

"Really?" Jessie asked.

Slater closed his eyes. "I'm getting a vision right now. I see . . . a gorgeous red-hot momma with long, curly hair and even longer legs cuddling up to me and whispering sweet nothings in my ear."

Jessie smirked. " 'Nothing' is exactly what you're

going to get, big fellow. And it sure won't be *sweet*."

"It doesn't look like you're much of a psychic, Slater," Zack pointed out.

Slater grinned. "I didn't say *when* it would happen. Jessie and I have a date tonight. Ask me tomorrow if I got any cuddling."

"Dream on," Jessie murmured, but she couldn't help melting a little when Slater gave her a cocky grin.

Just then, Lisa ran back to the booth in her bare feet. She tossed her brand-new pink leather sandals on the table. When they flew into Slater's catsup-filled plate, she didn't even wince. That's when the gang knew it was serious.

"Rosina is amazing!" Lisa declared, wonderment in her big, dark eyes. "She told me I'm going to be a famous fashion designer!"

Daintily, Zack picked up one of Lisa's catsup-splattered sandals by its strap. "You already have a head start," he said. "Look, a new trend—edible shoes."

"You'd have to deep-fry them first, Zack," Screech informed him gravely. "And I'd add some hot sauce, too."

Lisa looked down at her pink toenails with awe. "Who knew that toes could say so much?" she breathed.

"I'm next," Jessie announced, sliding out of the booth. "I've got to see this."

"But I already told your fortune!" Slater called after her. Jessie ignored him and headed toward the back booth and Rosina.

"I can't wait," Kelly said, taking a sip of her soda. "I'm sure Rosina will tell me everything I need to know about Cody."

Cody, Zack thought in despair, *Cody Durant, the surfer god. Mr. Perfect; Mr. Wonderful.*

Zack gazed at Kelly across the table and thought about her instead. She was so drop-dead gorgeous, it was a wonder he was still up and walking around. Her eyes were the blue of a desert sky. Her skin was flawless, lightly tanned with a few endearing freckles he knew by heart. Her great legs haunted his dreams, and her smile could light up Los Angeles. But the best part about Kelly, the part he really loved, was her heart. It was open, trusting, and honest. If sweetness were a town, Kelly would be Hershey, Pennsylvania.

"Zack, are you okay?" Kelly asked him worriedly. "You look kind of sick."

Zack almost groaned aloud. He was always thinking romantic thoughts about Kelly, but she treated him like a brother—a sad, pathetic little brother she had to watch out for. "Must be the onion rings," he said weakly.

"But you didn't have any," Slater pointed out.

Zack shot him a dirty look. "It was watching you eat them," he said. "That's enough to make anybody barf."

Jessie bounced back to the table, her wild curls flying. "Guess what?" she exclaimed. "Rosina says that an important man will come back into my life. She said he'll change it completely!"

"Big deal," Slater said. "That already happened. We got back together last week. She must be in a time warp."

"No," Jessie said, sitting down. "She said an *older* man. It's totally mysterious."

"Wow," Lisa said. "An *older* man. That sounds really romantic. Like Mel Gibson." When Slater gave her a hostile look, she said meekly, "Well, actually, it could be, like, George Burns, too."

"This is totally bogus," Slater said angrily. "It's so general. She's telling you just what you want to hear. I can't believe you girls are falling for this."

"I agree," Zack said. "Take it from a master scammer. Rosina is a champ."

"Make that chump, partner," Slater said, scowling.

"I think it's exciting," Kelly protested. "I'm going next. That is, if you don't want to go, Screech."

Screech shuddered. "Are you kidding? I can't even handle my *present*. My future might send me into shock."

"Maybe you shouldn't see Rosina, Kelly," Zack said. "You're so happy. Why spoil things?"

"She won't spoil anything," Kelly said, turning

her head to search the Max. "She'll just confirm things. Hey, where is she?"

The rest of them scanned the café, but there was no sign of the spangled, exotic Rosina. She had disappeared into thin air.

"I didn't see her leave," Slater said.

Kelly slumped against the table. "Oh, no. I really wanted my fortune told. I wanted to hear what she had to say about Cody."

"Maybe she'll be back tomorrow," Lisa said encouragingly.

Suddenly Zack had an idea. A scam. He'd promised himself he'd go easy on the scheming after he'd practically destroyed the school a few months ago on Student-Teacher Role-Reversal Day. He'd suspected that the Mud-Wrestling Festival in the gym was a bad idea, but he hadn't expected the principal, Mr. Belding, to get suspended because of it. After that fiasco, Zack had straightened out. He had been good for quite a while now. No wonder he was bored!

Was he going to let Kelly slip away because of a few scruples? Lisa had given him the perfect idea. Kelly wanted her fortune told. Well, didn't Zack know her fate better than anyone?

"You know, Kelly," he said thoughtfully. "Now that I think about it, you girls might be right. Rosina sounded like the real thing."

Slater raised an eyebrow at his friend, but he

didn't say anything. "But I'm never going to know my future," Kelly said glumly.

"Not until it gets here," Screech agreed. "But then it will be your present, so you still won't know your future."

"I'm totally disappointed," Kelly pouted.

Zack nodded sympathetically, but inside, he was grinning his widest grin. Good-bye, Snoresville, U.S.A. That old Zack magic was back!

Chapter 2

Late that afternoon, Zack raided his mother's closet. Luckily, his mother was a pack rat. She never threw anything away. Even though he had to push to the very back of the closet, he found what he was looking for. Back in her younger days, before Zack was born, Amelia Morris had been a hippie.

Zack pulled out long, dripping scarves and a tie-dyed chiffon skirt that would be about ankle-length on him. He even found some flowing scarves with spangles, just like Rosina's. Then he raided his mother's jewelry box and came up with a pile of silver bracelets and necklaces.

Zack bundled the loot under his arm and raced to his room. Within minutes, he had transformed himself into a gypsy. He wrapped a scarf around his head and penciled in a beauty mark near his mouth right where Rosina's was. Then he peered at himself in the mirror. He still somehow looked like Zack. It was his eyes. But Zack had his limits, and one of them was eyeliner. Instead, he slipped on Ray·Bans. Then he wrapped a scarf around the lower part of his face so you couldn't see his chin.

His parents weren't home, so it was no trouble to sneak out to the driveway and jump into his car. Zack left the top of his convertible up. He wasn't about to let people see him driving around like this. At least dusk was falling fast, and soon it would be dark.

When Zack got to Kelly's house, he parked the car halfway down the block, right underneath an overgrown pine tree that would probably drip sap on his new paint job. But at least the car would be concealed in the shadows.

Zack paused to give a last look in the rearview mirror. He had to admit he looked great. He squinted at his image. "Zere ees no such theeng as luck," he intoned. He pitched his voice lower and repeated it. He sounded just about perfect! Feeling brave and daring, Zack hiked up his chiffon skirt and walked to Kelly's.

He rang the bell, praying that Kelly would answer. Kelly had so many sisters and brothers that there was no telling who would answer the door and turn him away. If he rang his own doorbell dressed like this, he'd definitely tell himself to get lost.

But luck was with him. Kelly answered the door. She had changed from her school clothes into an old blue sweatshirt and blue leggings, and she looked as gorgeous as ever.

Her face brightened when she saw Zack, then a look of confusion crossed her face. "Rosina!" she said. "How did you find me?"

Zack pitched his voice very low. "Fate has brought me here to read your fortune. I had a vision."

"A vee-jon?" Kelly asked, puzzled.

"A vee-shun," Zack repeated. "You know." He waved his hands in the air in what he hoped was a mystical way.

"Oh, a *vision*," Kelly said, pleased. She opened the door wider. "Come on in."

"Thank you, my child," Zack said.

"We can use my father's study," Kelly said, leading the way down the hall. As she walked into the room, she put out a hand to turn on the light, since the room was in shadow.

"No light," Zack said quickly. When Kelly looked at him curiously, he said, "My visions come easier in the dark. Besides, I have an eye infection."

Kelly shrugged and left the light off. But she looked back at him. "But how will you be able to read my feet?"

"There is light enough where the spirit shines," Zack babbled.

Kelly seated herself in her father's old maroon leather armchair. Zack sat on the matching footstool. Kelly took her sock off and placed her foot in his lap. He held it up, peering at it.

Kelly giggled. "That tickles."

Zack wanted to laugh, too, but this was serious work. He frowned instead. "Your toes tell me you have found true love."

"They do?" Kelly asked breathlessly. "That's fantastic!"

"He is very close to you already," Zack said, tracing a line down the sole of Kelly's foot while she squirmed and giggled. "But you do not see him."

"That's true," Kelly said in amazement. She blushed. "He's at the beach all the time, right?"

She was thinking about Cody again! "No," Zack intoned, shaking his head. "I do not speak of the physical. I speak of the heart. You do not see him with your heart."

"Oh," Kelly said, puzzled. "I don't?"

Zack shook his head solemnly. "He is standing right beside you," he continued. "He has loved you long, and he has loved you well. There were times he was blind, and you were blind. Now he sees, and you do not."

Kelly gazed at him, enraptured. "What does he see?" she asked.

"He sees true love. He sees that you are the only

woman for him. Now you, too, must recognize this." Zack peeked at her. Kelly was leaning toward him, her mouth open, her eyes shining, hanging on his every word. "Your true love is your old love," Zack said in a low, throbbing tone. "You must recognize his face."

Kelly frowned. "Recognize his face? I thought I knew him."

"You know him, but you don't know him," Zack said. He was beginning to feel frustrated. He knew he shouldn't spell out what he was talking about. But if he didn't get more specific, Kelly wouldn't realize that he was talking about himself. "He is fair and handsome. Smart, with a quick tongue."

Kelly looked puzzled. "He has krypton? Isn't that what Superman is allergic to?"

"Not krypton," Zack barked impatiently. "A *queek tong*."

Suddenly the study door banged open. Kyle, one of Kelly's little brothers, stood on the threshold. Last year, when he'd been seven, he had enjoyed hiding behind the couch in the family room when Zack and Kelly were watching TV. Every time Zack had tried to kiss Kelly, Kyle had stood up and bopped him on the head with a pillow. He was eight now, and he'd only gotten worse.

"Who's that?" he asked, pointing at Zack.

"She's a gypsy," Kelly said impatiently. "She's telling my fortune. Go away, Kyle. We're busy."

Kyle rolled his eyes and came farther into the

room. "It doesn't look like a gypsy," he said. "It looks like a hippie."

"Kyle!" Kelly exclaimed, embarrassed. "Don't call Rosina an 'it.' And clear out, okay? I'll let you pick the TV programs tonight," she said in a wheedling voice.

Kyle tugged at Zack's scarf, and Zack dropped Kelly's foot, his heart pounding wildly. He snatched at his scarf before it fell off his head. Kelly's foot banged on the floor.

"Ow!" she said, rubbing her toes.

"So sorry, young lady," Zack said with a bow. "See? Sensitive foot. Easy to read."

Kyle tugged at his scarf again. "You're funny," he said. "I know you."

In another minute, Zack would be unmasked. "No, you don't, kid," he whispered fiercely. "And if you don't go away, I'll put a curse on you."

Kyle only stuck out his tongue and then tried to peer into Zack's face. Zack kept his head averted and began to back out of the room.

"Look, Kelly!" Kyle called out. "The gypsy's wearing running shoes!"

"I must go," Zack said frantically. "My spirit guides are calling."

Kelly rose. "Wait, I have to pay you—"

"No charge, miss. No charge. Aloha," Zack blurted, and ran down the hall before Kyle could get near him again.

He wrenched open the front door and dashed down the street, hoping Kelly wasn't looking out the window. The real Rosina definitely wasn't a sprinter type.

Zack jumped into his car with a sigh of relief. That had been a close one! But at least he'd been able to get through to Kelly. He'd told her her true love was an old love, fair haired, with a quick tongue. She'd have to know that it was Zack!

▲   ▼   ▲

"I just couldn't believe it," Kelly bubbled to Slater, Lisa, and Zack the next morning before school. "Rosina just came right out and said that my true love was Cody!"

Zack gulped. "Cody?" he practically squeaked.

"She did?" Lisa breathed. "How romantic!"

"Are you sure?" Zack asked.

Kelly nodded. "Absolutely. She said I'd known him for a long time. Well, I met Cody the summer before last. She said that I've loved him a long time, and it's been three whole months. And she said there were times when he was blind and I was blind. Cody didn't write to me for a whole year, and then when he came back into my life, I wasn't sure that he really loved me."

"Thanks to Zack," Lisa pointed out dryly. "He

was the one to rope Cody into his plan to embarrass
Ms. Martinet." Ms. Martinet was the horrible tem-
porary principal at Bayside High who had replaced
Mr. Belding. Zack had talked Cody into ignoring
Kelly so that he wouldn't alienate Ms. Martinet.

"Hey, I got them back together, didn't I?" Zack
protested. Sure he had. He had had to, or he'd have
lost Kelly's friendship forever.

"You're so lucky, Kelly," Lisa told her. "It must
really lessen the pressure to know that you've
picked the right guy at last."

Kelly nodded. "It's fantastic," she said.

"I don't know, Kelly," Zack said. "It sounds
pretty vague to me. How can you be so sure Rosina
was talking about Cody?"

"She said that he's fair," Kelly said. "That's
definitely Cody. The surfers at the beach all say
how he doesn't hog the waves."

"Right," Zack said hopelessly. He hadn't meant
fair. He'd meant *fair*. He'd meant himself!
"What else?"

"She said he's handsome," Kelly said dreamily.
"Oh, and that he has a quick tongue. I mean, isn't
that Cody to a tee?"

Slater rolled his eyes at Zack. Cody wasn't exactly the best conversationalist in the world. Only
Kelly would think he was witty.

"Sounds like him all right," Slater agreed gener-
ously. He wouldn't hurt Kelly's feelings if he could
help it.

Alarmed, Zack turned back to Kelly. "This woman is a crackpot!" he exclaimed. "You can't seriously think she's for real, can you?"

A cloud crossed Kelly's brow. "What do you mean, Zack? You were the one who said that she was the real thing, remember?"

Darn, he *had* said that. Zack met Kelly's gaze with honest hazel eyes. "I didn't say she was the real thing, Kelly," he lied. "I said she was a real *ding-a-ling*. She's obviously a complete fraud. How could any of her predictions ever come true?"

Just then, Jessie ran up to them excitedly, her curly hair bouncing. Her face was flushed, and she was hugging her books to her chest. "Guess what!" she exclaimed. "Rosina's prediction came true!"

"Great timing, Jessie," Zack said sourly.

"What is it?" Lisa demanded. "Did you met Mel Gib—I mean, George Burns?"

"My dad paid us a surprise visit last night," Jessie said. Jessie's father had been divorced from her mother for ten years. He was an executive at a luxury hotel in San Francisco, where he lived with his new young wife. "And guess what? He and Leslie have separated and he might be moving back to Palisades!"

"That's great, Jessie!" Kelly said. "I know how much you miss him."

"Well, it's not as great as meeting an incredible hunk, but it's good," Lisa said.

"I can't wait for you to meet him," Jessie said to Slater. "He's the greatest."

Lisa glanced at her watch. "I hate to break this up, gang, but I have to get to the girls' room and freshen up my makeup. I only have fifteen minutes before the bell."

"And I have to put my English paper in Mrs. Simpson's box," Slater said. "If it's not there this morning, my grade drops by a letter."

"I'll come with you," Jessie offered. "I want to tell you more about my dad."

Slater, Jessie, and Lisa headed off toward school, and Zack was left alone with Kelly. She gazed over his shoulder, scanning the parking lot for Cody's blue van.

"Listen, Kelly," Zack said hesitantly. "I have to say something to you—as a friend."

"Sure, Zack," Kelly said, still gazing out at the parking lot.

"It's about what Rosina told you," Zack said. "Kelly, even if you *think* you know your true love, you still can't put all your eggs in one basket. I mean, you can't live on bread alone. There's more than one flavor to Life Savers. And there's plenty of fish in the sea."

Kelly fixed him with quizzical blue eyes. "Zack, are you reciting a shopping list or do you have a point?"

Zack shook his head. "Kelly, Kelly, Kelly. You're

a *teenager*. You're young, free, and not even twenty-one. The teen years are a time of experimentation. Exploration. We're heading toward the rain forest of life, and you're reaching for the defoliant!"

"Zack," Kelly said impatiently, "you lost me back with the fish and the Life Savers. Get to the point."

Zack grasped Kelly's arms. "The point is that variety is the spice of life, Kelly. That's how we learn, how we grow. That's how we figure out what we want, and why. What kind of a life partner can you be for Cody if you don't experiment in your teenage years?"

Kelly nodded slowly. "I see what you're saying, Zack. But if I'm lucky enough to find out who my true love is, I can't just walk away."

"I'm not telling you to walk away," Zack said. He wished he could tell her to *run* away. "I'm telling you that it's best for you *and* Cody if you don't restrict yourself. Test your feelings. Experiment! Explore! It's the mature way to go, Kelly," he told her soberly.

"I'm sorry, Zack," Kelly said. "You could be right, but . . . I just can't follow your advice."

"Why not?" Zack asked. But Kelly wasn't looking at him anymore. Her gaze had wandered past his shoulder to the parking lot.

Zack turned. Cody was just swinging down from

his van. He swept his longish black hair off his shoulder with a casual hand as he slammed the van door shut with his foot and started across the parking lot. He was wearing a denim shirt and jeans that were faded to a soft, pale blue. He looked very tan next to the pale color, and when he smiled at a passing girl, his teeth flashed in the sunshine. The girl walked straight into a tree.

"That's why," Kelly said happily.

Chapter 3

In Zack's P.E. class that day, Coach Sonski announced basketball. Warm-ups were first, and Zack joined the line of guys waiting to do lay-ups. Cody Durant was in front of him, wearing gym shorts and a sweatshirt with cutoff arms. Zack watched as Cody caught the basketball easily and then drove toward the basket and executed a perfect lay-up.

Cody tossed the ball back to Zack, who caught it with only a slight "Oof." He dribbled toward the basket, then tossed the ball in an arc. It wobbled around the rim three times, then dropped away.

"Too bad, man," Cody said in a friendly way as Zack joined him at the end of the line.

"Basketball isn't my sport," Zack said.

"Mine, either," Cody replied. His fingers

drummed against his leg nervously, and he peered at Zack, then looked away.

"Something on your mind, Cody?" Zack asked. He hoped Cody wasn't going to confide in him again about Kelly. Zack had become Cody's confidant a couple of weeks ago when the two had been having trouble, and it had been agony.

"It's Kelly," Cody said. He looked around nervously. Coach Sonski was at the other end of the court, arranging a passing drill. "Can I talk to you, Zack?" Cody said in a low voice.

No, you girlfriend-stealing, muscle-flexing hunk of perfection. "Sure," Zack said.

"You know her, right?" Cody said. "You were her dude and all. And you might be able to help me, sort of."

"Me?" Zack asked incredulously. "Help you? Um, I mean, what do you have in mind, Cody?"

"Kelly is real romantic," Cody confided. "So I take her out to this place by the beach the other night. A nice place. Real napkins. I mean, they even gave you menus, Zack. You didn't order at a counter or anything. I'm talking *class.*"

"I get the picture." Zack nodded gravely.

"So I'm holding her hand and we're looking at the waves, and she's staring at me. And I know that she's waiting for me to tell her stuff."

"Stuff?" Zack asked.

"Romantic stuff. About her eyes and junk. How

pretty she is. How much I'm nuts about her. You know, *stuff.*"

Zack nodded. "Oh, right. *Stuff.*"

Cody sighed. "You might not believe this, Zack. I know it might be hard to accept and all. But with girls, I'm not the same witty talker that I am around guys."

"No!" Zack exclaimed. "You're kidding."

"No," Cody assured him, moving up to the head of the line. Bucky Finelli was dribbling down the court for his lay-up. "I swear. It's a brain-drain thing. It's like I'm stupid or something." Just then, Bucky tossed the basketball to Cody, and it bonked him in the head.

Cody looked sheepish as he retrieved the ball. He bounced it toward the basket for his lay-up. The ball swished in.

Zack caught the ball and concentrated hard as he drove toward the basket. He tossed the ball, but it hit the backboard and careened off to the side.

"Anyway," Cody continued as Zack reached the end of the line, "as I was saying, I'm just not cool around girls I like. And I'm really freaked that it's starting to bother Kelly."

"I don't know what to tell you, Cody," Zack said. "I guess you just have to loosen up. Try pretending she's a guy."

Cody thought about this. "I can't do that, Zack. I mean, no guy has legs like Kelly."

"That's for sure," Zack muttered fervently.

"So I was thinking that I'd *write* to her. It's the perfect solution, man. A love letter. I don't think Kelly's ever really forgiven me for not writing to her after we met two summers ago."

"Letters are good," Zack said, nodding. "Girls just eat 'em up." Giving Cody advice was a piece of cake. All Zack had to do was agree and nod a lot.

Cody's head bobbed enthusiastically. "I'm glad you said that. Because I want you to write one for me."

Zack stared at him in amazement. "You want me to *what*?"

"I want you to write a love letter to Kelly for me," Cody said patiently.

"I heard you," Zack said. "I just don't believe what I'm hearing."

"Well, I can't write it!" Cody said defensively. "Look, Zack, you've got the gift, man. You know what to say to girls. You know what makes them melt. So I thought maybe in exchange for surfing tips, you could write a letter. All you have to do is pretend you're still in love with Kelly. It's simple."

"Simpler than you think," Zack murmured.

"Huh?"

"Nothing."

"You'd be the most incredibly cool dude in the universe if you'd do this, Zack," Cody told him solemnly. "You're the only one who can help me."

Zack thought hard. It was probably a really bad idea. Write a letter to Kelly so that she'd fall even harder for this surfing stud? It just didn't make sense.

Unless you applied a whole new system of logic. *Cody and Kelly plus Zack Morris could equal one happy pair*, Zack thought. And he didn't mean Kelly and Cody. It would just take a little scheming. If anyone could turn a negative situation into a positive one, it was Zack. He probably could win Kelly back from Cody if he was right in the middle of the two of them.

Cody executed another lay-up. This time, the ball missed the hoop completely. He ran after it sheepishly, then flipped the ball back to Zack.

Zack bounced the ball a few times and eyed the net. He told himself that his luck would start to change right now if he made the right moves. Without moving any closer, he tossed the ball in a stunning arc all the way across the gym floor. It swished through the net without even touching the rim.

"All *right!*" everyone yelled.

"Way to go, Morris!" Coach Sonski shouted from the other end of the gym.

Zack jogged toward Cody, grinning. "I'll do it!" he told him. Cody reached out to give him a high five. *Yes,* Zack thought, slapping Cody's palm in

satisfaction. *This'll be the way to win Kelly back.*
How can anything go wrong?

▲   ▼   ▲

That night Slater arranged his very own fantasy
evening. He had the beach. He had the full moon.
He had the blanket and the boom box with a knap-
sack full of romantic tapes. The only thing missing
was the girl.

Jessie was with him, all right. But every time he
moved in for a little romantic action, she started
talking about her father. It was really putting the
damper on Slater. After all, what kind of a girl
would think about any other man when Slater was
around?

"Look at the moon," Slater said softly. He gently
guided Jessie back until she was leaning on her
elbows, looking up at the night sky.

"It's beautiful," Jessie said in a hushed voice.
She twisted around and looked deeply into his eyes.
"Did I ever tell you that my father wanted to be an
astronomer?"

"Fascinating," Slater said. "Your eyes look beautiful in the moonlight, Jessie."

"Thanks." Jessie smiled softly at him, and he
moved in for the kill. Their lips were almost touching when she suddenly sprang forward. Slater fell
back on the blanket in despair.

"You know, this would be a great place for my mom and dad to spend some time together," Jessie mused. "It's a terrific place to just get away from everything and talk, isn't it?"

"Talking wasn't what I had in mind," Slater grumbled.

"Last night I heard them talking in the living room after I went upstairs to bed," Jessie said. "I even heard my mom laugh. She *never* laughs when she's talking to my dad."

"Mmmm," Slater said. He reached out a hand and began to run his fingers through Jessie's long, gorgeous hair.

Jessie wriggled a little bit backward in appreciation, but she remained upright, staring at the moon-silvered ocean. "I guess they just needed some time to see each other's point of view," she said thoughtfully. "I know what that's like."

"Me, too," Slater agreed. He sat up and slipped his arm around Jessie. "We were like that once. Fighting all the time. Never again, right?"

Jessie nodded. "Never. I mean, we have a much more mature relationship now. And we're really *together*, you know?"

"Totally in sync," Slater agreed. He took Jessie's chin in his hand and gently turned her head so that she was facing him. "Every day, I feel closer to you," he said softly. Jessie's hazel eyes turned smoky, and her mouth parted. He felt a sigh drift past his cheek. Slater leaned in and kissed her.

Finally! Jessie responded to the kiss, and Slater slipped both arms around her. Her lips were soft and curved under his invitingly. Now things were really getting started. He was in for some serious cuddling with his number one sweetie.

They broke the kiss, and Slater ran a finger down the curve of her cheek. "You are some gorgeous package, momma," he murmured.

"Oh, Slater," Jessie murmured throatily. "Do you think my parents could really get back together?"

Slater slammed a hand down on the blanket. "That's it!" he said. "I've had it. Jessie, are you here with me, or are you still home with your parents? Because if you're here right now, you're giving a pretty good imitation of someone who doesn't want to be."

Jessie stiffened. "Wait a second," she said angrily. "Let me get this straight. Something super-important is going on in my life, and all you care about is getting your full love quotient for the night!"

"That's not true," Slater sputtered. "I just want to be with you. Not you and the whole Spano family!"

Jessie sprang to her feet. "Well, thanks a lot. Now I know who to come to when I need some understanding. Anybody but you!"

Slater rose in one quick motion. "What's that

supposed to mean?" he demanded hotly.

"It means that you don't even want to listen to me!" Jessie shouted. Suddenly, her eyes filled with tears. "What do you know about it, anyway? You've always had a family. Your dad never left you. You don't know what it's like to want a family so bad—" Jessie choked, and she couldn't go on.

Slater felt instantly contrite. "Aw, Jessie, I'm sorry. Come on. Sit down and we can talk."

Jessie's eyes flashed. "Forget it. I've learned my lesson. I'll never confide in you again, A. C. Slater. And if you think I'll ever kiss you again, you're positively deranged!" Tossing her curls, Jessie ran up the beach.

Quickly Slater bent down and gathered up the blanket and boom box. He had to stop Jessie from trying to walk home in the dark. The girl was crazy enough to do something like that.

Slater sighed. So much for the new, improved version of their relationship. It looked like he and Jessie were back to the same old fireworks display. Once Slater had loved their constant sparring— every day was like the Fourth of July. But even a true-blue patriot didn't mind a day off now and then. And Slater wanted Jessie to know how much he really cared—a lot.

Chapter 4

Dear Kelly,

You might think it's weird getting a letter from me. After all, I see you every day. But there are so many things in my heart that there aren't enough hours in the day to express them out loud. I thought it would be easier to write them, but now I'm staring at the page and I don't know where to start. What would Mrs. Simpson say?

Okay. She'd say, "Organize your main points in order of importance, Mr. Durant." But I only have one point, and it's really simple. I love you, Kelly. Even when I talk about school or catching a wave, I'm really thinking how pretty you are. And when I tell you how blue the ocean is, I'm really thinking of your eyes.

Love,

Cody

Kelly pressed her lips to the letter. Then she tied a lilac ribbon around it and placed it underneath her pillow. She crawled under the covers and gazed out the window. A full moon was rising, and she sighed as she looked at it.

She had never felt so perfectly, blissfully happy. The tiny worry about Cody that had been nagging at her had been dispelled. There were times, she could admit now, that she hungered for a more romantic Cody. He usually talked about surfing or sports, and sometimes she even could get the teensiest bit bored. She'd just zone out, staring at his clear green eyes and great shoulders while Cody droned on about every wave he'd caught that morning before school. Kelly hadn't liked to admit it to herself, but she had wondered if Cody had a romantic bone in his body.

And now it turned out that he was the most romantic guy ever. Even more romantic than Zack! Zack had teased and kidded her, but in his serious moments, he had made her feel like the most beautiful girl alive. Now it turned out that Cody was every bit as romantic as Zack—even more so!

And when I tell you how blue the ocean is, I'm really thinking of your eyes. . . .

Kelly smiled as she began to drift off to sleep. She thought of how great tomorrow would be, the secret smiles and glances that would pass between her and Cody. Now she knew his secret soul.

Cody wasn't just another gorgeous surfer—he was a poet!

▲   ▼   ▲

The next morning at school, Jessie stood talking to Lisa, trying not to look for Slater. She had still been furious when he'd dropped her off at her house the night before, and there was no way she'd spend even one second wondering about the whereabouts of that curly headed, adorable jerk. When it came to emotions, he was somewhere around caveman level, and he had spent last night proving it.

"What's the matter, Jessie?" Lisa asked. "You keep twisting around. Are you practicing a new dance, or are you looking for Slater?"

Jessie shook her head. "Neither. I have a—uh— stiff neck."

"Too cold at the beach last night?" Lisa asked with an impish grin.

Just then Slater came up behind Jessie. "Way too cold," he said. "Freezing, in fact."

"Didn't you keep her warm, Slater?" Lisa asked him. "That's your job."

Jessie tossed her head. "I was fine. Lisa, we should get to class."

For the first time, Lisa realized that something

was wrong between Jessie and Slater. She shivered. "Brrrrr. Speaking of cold temperatures, are you two fighting again?"

"We're not fighting," Jessie said evenly. "I'm much too mature to fight. It's just that I've recently come to realize that I'm dating a Neanderthal with dimples."

Slater turned to Lisa. "So sue me if I wanted her undivided attention last night. I tried to apologize, but you know Ms. Spano. She acted like I'd thrown all my plastic recyclables out on the side of the highway."

"That bad," Lisa said sympathetically.

"I mean, what do I have to do—grovel?" Slater groused.

Lisa saw the gleam in Jessie's eyes. "You know, Slater," she said as she adjusted her skirt, "I think that might be the way to go."

"Hey, I grovel for no woman," Slater said, crossing his muscular arms. Lisa gave him a meaningful look, and he sighed. "Except *my* woman," he added helplessly.

Slowly Slater sank to his knees. "Jessie, I was wrong. Please forgive me," he said. "This is a totally sincere grovel."

Jessie batted at him, embarrassed. "Slater, get up. I don't want you to grovel."

"But I'm so good at it," Slater protested.

Jessie pressed her lips together to hide a grin.

"Why should I forgive you?" she asked. "All I ask is that you be interested in my mind, not just my body."

Still on his knees, Slater moved a bit closer to her. "If you want me to be interested in your mind, momma, don't take me to a deserted beach with a full moon."

One corner of Jessie's mouth lifted, but she tried to frown. "I don't know what to do," she said, barely able to suppress a giggle when Slater put his curl-covered head against her knee and looked up at her with pleading soft, brown eyes.

"If I were you, I'd forgive him," Lisa said flatly. "If you don't do it soon, we're going to have to spread newspapers on the floor."

Jessie patted Slater's head. "I forgive you. Now get up before Lisa gives you a dog biscuit."

"All right, already," Slater said, rising and dusting off his knees. "I'm not your very own puppy dog, you know."

"I know," Jessie said. She leaned over and kissed him on the nose. "But your nose *is* kind of cold and wet."

Slater took a menacing step closer to her. "Don't push it, Spano," he growled. He leaned over and gave her a smacking kiss on the lips. Then he barked at her.

Lisa rolled her eyes. "You guys had better cut out the sweet stuff. It's bad for my complexion."

Jessie snuggled closer into Slater's arms. "I'm so glad we made up," she said.

"Me, too," Slater agreed. "Making up is the best part of an argument. Especially if we go back to the beach," he added with a devilish grin.

"I have a better way to make up," Jessie said. "I want you to come to dinner tonight and meet my father."

Slater gulped. Meeting Mr. Spano was not exactly his idea of a romantic evening, but he wasn't about to make *that* mistake again. "Sounds great," he said firmly.

Jessie cocked a flirtatious eyebrow at him. "And after that," she said, her eyes twinkling, "we can go to the beach."

▲   ▼   ▲

Cody cornered Zack by his locker. "It worked, man," he told him in a low tone. "You're a genius. Kelly thinks I'm the most romantic guy since . . . since, like, Don . . ."

"Juan?" Zack finished.

"Johnson," Cody finished. "Who's Don Juan? I can't keep track of these actors nowadays."

"He's not an actor," Zack explained. "He's a famous romantic guy. Like Casanova."

"Casa Nova?" Cody repeated the name. "Is that

that new Mexican restaurant on Ocean Parkway?"

Zack patted Cody on the shoulder. "Forget it, Cody. I was glad to help." Actually, Zack had enjoyed writing the letter to Kelly. He'd been able to spill on paper all the things he'd wanted to say to her face. While he was writing, he'd forgotten all about Cody. It had been a complete shock when Cody had taken the paper, recopied the letter, and signed his name. Zack had been left with a funny feeling in his stomach.

"See you around," Zack said. "Good luck with Kelly."

"Wait a second, man," Cody said, hurrying after him. "What about today?"

Zack stopped. "What about it?"

"You have to write another one," Cody said. "I told Kelly I'd write her a letter every day."

"You *what*?" Zack said incredulously.

"I told Kelly I'd write—"

"I heard you!" Zack roared. A couple of students turned and looked at him, and he lowered his voice. "Cody, why did you do that? I can't write Kelly every day!"

"Why not?"

"Because . . . Well, because I'll get writer's cramp," Zack improvised. He shook his hand and winced. "With all the writing I have to do in school—and writing to Kelly—I don't know. Last night I had to do draft after draft until it was absolutely perfect. It was rough, Cody."

"Why don't you use a typewriter?" Cody suggested. "That would be easier for me, too, because then I wouldn't have to recopy it. I'm not good at penmanship, either."

Zack shook his head. "Look, Cody, I was glad to help you out once. But I can't make a regular thing of it." *That would be agony,* Zack thought.

"Come on, Zack. You've just got to. All of a sudden, Kelly thinks I'm a real romantic dude. You should have heard her go on and on about the part where I said when I was talking about the ocean, I was really thinking about her eyes. That was inspired, man. She thinks I'm a poet. I mean, she thinks *you're* a poet. You can't stop now."

"A poet, huh," Zack mused. Kelly had never called him a poet. He had to admit he was flattered. Of course, now she'd said it about Cody. But somehow, it felt pretty good, anyway.

"All right," Zack said finally. "I'll do a couple more. But that's it." He could force himself to pour out his heart to his one and only love, his destiny, his fate, his Kelly. . . .

"Who is *that*?" Zack blurted to Cody as a curvaceous knockout with a wild head of flaming red hair walked by. She was dressed in a classy but formfitting black minidress, and she gave Zack a long look with glittering topaz eyes that were rimmed with long, spiky lashes. "Wow," Zack breathed.

"You said it, man," Cody agreed, watching the girl make her sinuous way down the hall. "She must

be the new transfer student. I hear she's from
Europe. Or maybe France, I don't remember."

"Wow," Zack said. It wasn't often he was at a
loss for words. But Mademoiselle VaVaVa Voom
had knocked every coherent thought out of his
head.

"So can you write the letter tonight?" Cody
urged.

"Sure," Zack said. "I'll put it in Kelly's locker
tomorrow." Zack's scheming mind was already
hard at work. After he poured his heart out to
Kelly, he'd be ready to take on new projects, new
interests. As long as Kelly was head over heels for
Cody, Zack didn't have to sit by idly. His first new
project would be to become a one-man welcoming
committee for the new transfer student at Bayside
High. *Its the least I can do*, he thought. The poor
girl seemed awfully shy.

Chapter 5

That night Slater arrived at Jessie's house and walked slowly up the steps to the front door. He had to admit he was nervous. He usually felt at ease in social situations, but Jessie was so excited about this dinner and about him getting along with her dad that his nerves were completely shot.

When Jessie opened the door, he felt better immediately. Just the sight of his gorgeous girlfriend could cure anyone. She looked fantastic in a red miniskirt and a black sweater with black tights and black suede boots.

"Whoa," Slater murmured. "Are you sure you want to look so hot when we have to eat with your parents? I'm probably going to drop roast beef in my lap."

"We're having chicken," Jessie said, smiling. "Come on in."

"Sorry I'm late," Slater said. "My dad had to work late, so I sat with my mom while she ate dinner. She gets lonesome when she has to eat alone."

"That was sweet of you," Jessie said.

"Don't you know that I'm a sweet guy at heart?" Slater murmured, sliding his arm around her waist. "Or do I have to show you all the time?"

Jessie batted his arm away, laughing. "Behave yourself. And come meet my dad."

Slater walked into the living room. Mr. Spano was standing by the fireplace, a drink in his hand. He was dressed in a gray suit and a silk tie of muted violets and grays. A little formal for a dinner at home, Slater thought. Maybe he should have worn a tie, too. He'd worn his best sweater, though.

"Dad," Jessie said proudly, "I'd like you to meet A. C. Slater. Slater, this is my dad, Alex Spano."

Slater shook his hand. "I'm glad to meet you, Mr. Spano."

"Glad to meet you . . . Slater? Isn't that what Jessie calls you?"

Slater nodded.

"Do you have a first name?" Mr. Spano queried.

"Sure. A," Slater joked. "And my middle name is C."

Mr. Spano gave a slight smile. "Jessie, why don't you offer Slater a soda or a glass of juice?"

"I'll have whatever you're having," Slater said to

Jessie. With despair, he watched her leave the room. Now he'd have to make conversation with Mr. Spano. But he'd already thought of his opening question. "What are you doing in Palisades, sir?" he asked.

"Visiting my daughter, mostly," Mr. Spano replied. "And I'm doing some business with the Palisades Beach Resort Hotel. The hotel I work for is part of a chain, and we're thinking of acquiring this one, too. I hope the deal goes through. That way I'll get to see Jessie more. San Francisco is just too far away."

"I know Jessie would like that, too," Slater agreed.

"And what are your interests, Slater?" Mr. Spano asked.

"Sports," Slater replied cheerfully. "I'm captain of the football team, but I'd have to say that my real love is wrestling."

"Ah," Mr. Spano said. "Do you have a nickname? I've seen that Hulk person, I think."

"You're thinking of professional wrestling, sir," Slater said politely. "Amateur wrestling is different. Actually, it's more professional than professional wrestling, if you know what I mean."

"I see. And what else are you interested in?"

"Jessie," Slater admitted with a grin. But in a moment, he realized that his remark had gone over like a lead balloon.

"Are you interested in politics, the environment, theater?" Mr. Spano asked, naming Jessie's interests.

"Theater, sure," Slater said, seizing on the last item. "I love movies."

Mr. Spano's lips pressed together. "How about modern art?"

"I've got some neat posters in my room at home," Slater offered. He felt like he was drowning.

He was saved when Jessie came back in, carrying two glasses of tomato juice. She handed one to Slater. "If you're trying to find out if Slater and I have anything in common, don't bother, Daddy," she said, shooting a fond glance at Slater. "Somehow we manage to have fun, though."

"You said it, momma," Slater said enthusiastically. Then he caught a glimpse of Jessie's father's face, and he said, "What I mean is, Jessie is a very, uh, stimulating intellectual companion."

Mr. Spano only grunted.

There was an awkward pause. Then Jessie's mother appeared in the doorway. She was a tall, willowy woman with short, light brown hair and a winning smile. "Slater! How are you, sweetheart?" she asked cheerfully.

At least Jessie's mom was crazy about him. "Great, Mrs. Spano. What smells so delicious?"

"Roast chicken with rosemary and garlic," Mrs.

Spano said with a grin. "It's my only domestic accomplishment." Mrs. Spano was a public defender, and Slater knew she worked like a fiend. Since Jessie wasn't much of a cook, either, the two of them ate more than their share of take-out. At least if Mr. Spano came back, they might eat better. Jessie had told Slater that her father was a fabulous cook.

"I think it's ready," Mrs. Spano went on. "So let's head to the table, shall we?"

"It smells great, Katie," Mr. Spano said warmly. He put a hand on Mrs. Spano's back as they left the living room.

"That's because you helped," Mrs. Spano said with a bright laugh.

Jessie gave Slater a significant look, and Slater raised his eyebrows. From what Jessie had told him, it did seem as though her parents were getting along better than they ever had, including when they were married.

Slater tugged on the bottom of Jessie's sweater as she followed her parents toward the dining room. She stopped in her tracks and turned to look at him.

"What is it?" she asked.

Slater waited until her parents were definitely out of earshot. "Jessie," he whispered, "your father hates me."

"Don't be ridiculous," Jessie whispered back. "He doesn't even know you yet. How could he hate you?"

"He thinks I'm a cross between Hulk Hogan and Jughead," Slater said despairingly.

Jessie giggled. "Well, if the shoe fits. . . ."

"Jessie, I'm not kidding," Slater's eyes had a pleading look. "This dinner party is the *Titanic*, and I'm the one who's going down with the ship."

Jessie patted his arm reassuringly. "You're being paranoid," she told him. "I'm sure my dad is going to love you just as much as I do. And besides, he's too busy thinking about my mom to worry about who I'm dating. Come on, let's go eat."

Slater's feet felt like lead as he followed Jessie to the dining room. For her sake, he wanted the Spanos to get back together. But if they did, he just might be dead meat. Slater shuddered as he had a sudden vision of the Spanos' next dinner party. The silver dish cover would be lifted, steam would rise, and Mr. Spano's signature dish, surrounded by sprigs of parsley, would be revealed: Slater's head.

▲   ▼   ▲

The next day at school, Zack arrived early and went straight to Mr. Belding's office. It was definitely a change to go there voluntarily. Usually Mr. Belding was the one to command Zack's presence, and it wasn't because the principal enjoyed chatting with him. From Zack alone, Mr. Belding's carpet had a worn spot in front of the desk. Zack found himself standing there more than the rest of the students combined.

Zack knocked on the door and stuck his head around it before Mr. Belding could answer. He gave him a dazzling smile. "Good morning, Mr. Belding."

Mr. Belding winced. His usually bland, pleasant face was creased in a deep frown. "Please, Morris, not today. I already *have* a headache. Whatever aggravation you're going to cause, can't it wait until tomorrow?"

Zack strolled into the office. "Aggravation? Mr. Belding, I just came to say hello."

"That's all?" Mr. Belding asked suspiciously.

Zack nodded virtuously. "That's all. I was just thinking this morning how awful it is that no one ever drops by to say hi. So I thought, *Zack, it's up to you.* So, hi, Mr. Belding."

"Hi, Zack," Mr. Belding answered patiently. "Now go away."

"Sure." Zack started toward the door. When his hand was on the knob, he hesitated.

Mr. Belding closed his eyes. "Please, no," he prayed.

"There's just one little thing," Zack said.

"No," Mr. Belding said. "No, no, and no."

"I didn't ask yet," Zack pointed out.

"You didn't have to," Mr. Belding said. "What-

ever your request is going to be, I already know it
will be inappropriate, outrageous, and possibly in-
decent. So, no."

"Well, how do you like that," Zack said. "I come
here to do *you* a favor, to support Bayside High,
and you won't even listen." He sighed.

Mr. Belding winced again. "What is it?" he
asked through gritted teeth.

"I know how hard you work, sir, to get that
family feeling here at Bayside," Zack told him.
"For instance, when Cody Durant transferred
here, you assigned him a student to help him
through the transition. I applaud that idea, Mr.
Belding. It makes a new student feel welcome. And
that's why I'd like to volunteer to help the next
transfer student adjust to a new school."

Mr. Belding nodded slowly. "You wouldn't have
happened to have seen a new transfer student
around, would you, Zack?"

Zack shook his head. "I heard there was someone," he said with a shrug. "But I haven't seen
her yet."

"So this new spirit of volunteerism would have
nothing to do with wanting to *date* the new student,
would it?" Mr. Belding asked.

Zack put a hand on his heart. "Mr. Belding, I am
shocked—shocked!—that you think I have an ulte-
rior motive. All I want is to uphold the welcoming
spirit and family atmosphere here at Bayside.

These things create a shining example for all of us, and should never, ever be tarnished by those cynics who would deny the pure hearts and deep feelings of those of us who—"

Mr. Belding looked at his watch. "Are you going to finish that sentence anytime soon, Zack? Because I have work to do. And the answer is no."

"But Mr. Belding—"

"I have asked Ms. Del Olio if she would like a student to help her through her first week here, and she has declined. She's a very sophisticated young lady, and she's used to adjusting to new schools. Her father is a diplomat, and I believe she is accustomed to new situations. End of issue. Goodbye, Zack."

"But—"

"Good-bye," Mr. Belding said with conviction. Zack knew from experience when a conversation was over. And this one definitely was. "Tell Mrs. Gibbs to bring me two aspirin on your way out, will you?"

"If she needs a locker, she can share mine," Zack offered. "I know how tight locker space is, Mr. Belding."

"Make that three aspirin," Mr. Belding said.

Zack passed the message on to Mrs. Gibbs, then headed for his locker. There just had to be a way to meet Ms. Del Olio. At least now he knew her name. He paused by Kelly's locker and quickly slipped in his latest love letter. When he turned away, Slater was just rounding the corner. And with that snake in the grass was the new transfer student!

She looked sophisticated and alluring in a short navy jacket and matching short skirt. She definitely looked older than the other girls. And she was looking at Slater as though he were the king of Bayside High. Zack had better blast his way into this conversation before Slater flashed his dimples and managed to get the new girl in a wrestling hold. Besides, wasn't Slater going steady with Jessie these days?

"Hey, Slater," Zack said, coming up to them. "How was meeting Jessie's father last night?"

"A disaster," Slater said cheerfully. "Zack, meet our newest transfer student, Dolores Del Olio. Dolores, this is Bayside High's biggest troublemaker, Zack Morris."

Zack gave Dolores his trademark thousand-watt smile. "Well, hello," he said warmly. "Welcome to Bayside High."

A small frown appeared between Dolores's eyebrows. "Troublemaker?"

Zack smiled and looked deeply into her gorgeous topaz eyes. "Don't listen to Slater. I prefer scam master."

"Zack turned the school completely upside down during Student-Teacher Role-Reversal Day,"

Slater volunteered. "You should have seen the gym after the Mud-Wrestling Festival!"

"Oh, my," Dolores said. Zack knew she was impressed with his great looks *and* the Wacky Wednesday mayhem. He could tell by the breathless tone in her voice.

"That was nothing compared to when the microwave ovens exploded," Zack added modestly.

"Marshmallow goo all over the second floor!" Slater hooted.

"I didn't know Bayside High was so . . . exciting," Dolores said.

"Oh, it's the most exciting place around," Zack said, moving in for the kill. "Why don't you let me show it to you?"

Dolores backed away. "I don't think so," she said nervously. "I have to go now. It was nice meeting you boys," she added. "Maybe I'll see you around."

With a deep frown, Zack watched Dolores go.

"Looks like the Morris cannonball was a dud," Slater said with a snicker. "She couldn't get away fast enough."

"I don't get it," Zack said. "Where did I go wrong?"

Slater shrugged. "Maybe she thought you weren't sophisticated enough," he guessed. "I was just talking to her about Europe. She's been everywhere. Her favorite place is Monte Carlo. Her last boyfriend was a race-car driver. She spends her holidays in Switzerland. Somehow I can't see her being attracted to the scam master of Bayside High, can you?"

"So we got off on the wrong foot," Zack said. "I have my sophisticated side, too, you know."

Slater guffawed. "Yeah—when you order a hot dog *without* chili on it, right?" Still laughing, Slater headed off down the hall.

Slater thinks his own jokes are hysterical, Zack thought irritably. But he did have a point. There had to be another way to get to Dolores.

Maybe Zack could arrange a little fortune-telling by Rosina—pull the same scam on Dolores. But, no, there was no way he'd put on those bracelets again. They'd given him a rash, and he hadn't been very convincing as a gypsy, anyway. Besides, he'd have no respect for himself in the morning if he used the same scam twice.

Then, suddenly, the most brilliant scheme Zack had ever concocted burst into his brain in all its glory. He snapped his fingers. He could leave off the bracelets and the skirt. But there was something *else* of Rosina's that could come in very handy when it came to wooing Dolores Del Olio.

Chapter 6

Slater looked for Jessie all day, but she was nowhere to be found. She didn't go to her locker in the morning, and she didn't eat lunch in the cafeteria. Once or twice, he thought he'd caught a glimpse of curly hair in the crowded hall, but after he'd pushed through the sauntering students, Jessie was gone—if she'd ever been there.

By the end of the school day, Slater was at the peak of frustration. He had a nagging fear that Jessie was avoiding him because of her father. Slater waited by her locker for fifteen minutes, but Jessie didn't show up.

Finally he gave up and started toward the door. He had promised his mother he'd run an errand for her downtown, so he couldn't wait for Jessie forever. His mom had bought a new dress that was being altered, and Slater had promised to pick it up.

As he pushed through the doors of school, he saw Jessie hurrying down the walk. With her long-legged gait and flying hair, Jessie was always easy to spot.

Slater called her name and hurried after her. Jessie appeared not to hear him, but when he called again, she stopped. Then she slowly turned around as he approached.

"Where have you been all day, Jess?" he asked in concern. "I've been trying to track you down."

Jessie shrugged. "I had a real busy day," she said evasively. She was wearing sunglasses, so he couldn't see her eyes.

"Are you all right?" Slater asked, peering at her.

Jessie passed a hand through her hair. "I'm fine. Listen, I have to go, so—"

"Wait a second." Slater grabbed her arm, and the sunglasses slipped a bit down Jessie's nose. Her eyes were cloudy and bloodshot. "Hey," Slater said softly. "Have you been crying, sweetheart?"

Jessie's mouth trembled. "Oh, Slater. My parents had a huge argument last night. I'm afraid they'll never get back together now!"

"But they seemed fine at dinner," Slater said, baffled.

"It was after dinner," Jessie said in a low tone. "My father . . ." Her voice trailed off, and she looked away.

"Your father what?" Slater prodded. "Did it

have something to do with me? You can tell me, Jessie."

"He didn't like you very much," Jessie said in a small voice. "I mean, it was nothing personal. But he thinks I could do better."

"That's not personal?" Slater asked, aggrieved. "Just what does he have against me?"

"Well," Jessie said, sniffing, "he thinks that you're just out for a good time."

"What's wrong with that?"

"Well, nothing. But Dad said that it's obvious that you have no serious interests. That you're just a jock. He says that we have nothing in common and that I could do much better—I mean, I could find someone more compatible. He didn't like that you were late for dinner. And he thought your hair was too long."

"Anything else?" Slater asked sarcastically.

Jessie hesitated. "Well," she added, "he hated your sweater."

Irritation coursed through Slater, but he tried to be patient. "What did you say?"

"I defended you, of course," Jessie said. "So did my mom. That's why they fought. Mom said that Dad had no right to dictate to me. And he said that he was just showing a concern that she should have, too. And she said . . . oh, never mind," Jessie sobbed. "It doesn't matter. The whole thing is hopeless."

Jessie's eyes slid away from his, and suddenly,

foreboding snaked through Slater. "Hey," he said, "you don't blame me for this, do you?"

"Of course not," Jessie returned uneasily. "But if you hadn't come to dinner, it wouldn't have happened."

"But you *asked* me to come to dinner!" Slater exploded.

"Well, you didn't have say yes!" Jessie said illogically. Then she burst into tears. "And you didn't have to wear that sweater!"

"Jessie, your mother is right," Slater said determinedly. "Your father has no right to lay down the law at this point. He practically disappeared from your life for years. I know you love him, but—"

"He's just trying to watch out for me," Jessie said, wiping her eyes and putting her sunglasses back on. "Look, he may be coming on too strong. But he's trying to be a father, and I can't fault him for that."

"Are you saying that you're going to *obey* him?" Slater thundered.

"Of course not!" Jessie said quickly. "But I don't want to antagonize him, either. Not to mention that I don't want Mom and Dad to fight again. So . . ."

Slater's face was stony. "So?"

"So maybe we could just . . . cut back on seeing each other, just a little bit." When Jessie saw Slater's face, she hurriedly added, "Just for a week or maybe two. That's all."

"That's all," Slater said flatly.

"Right," Jessie said nervously.

"Fine," Slater said in the same flat tone. But fury pulsed in his veins. "Maybe we should go all the way, Jessie. Let's do what Daddy wants. Let's not see each other at all."

Slater turned on his heels and stalked away. He heard Jessie calling him, tears in her voice, but he didn't turn around. Finally her voice just faded away.

▲   ▼   ▲

Zack had a surfing lesson scheduled with Cody at the beach, but he canceled it as soon as he got there.

"Something's come up, Cody," he told him. "Maybe we can do it on Saturday."

"Sure," Cody agreed. "I'm glad you came down to the beach, though. I wanted to talk to you about Kelly."

"Something wrong?" Zack asked. "I thought she was thrilled with the letters."

Cody looked uncomfortable. "Well, yeah. But I was thinking that maybe we should cool it a little. I mean, it's like she's getting more in love with me by the day. And it's not *me*, you know?"

"Sure it is," Zack reassured him. "I'm just putting into words how you feel."

Cody looked away down the beach. "Yeah, well.

Anyway. Phew. You know what I mean?"

"Sure I do, Cody," Zack agreed patiently. Sometimes conversing with the guy was like dropping into a language class in Urdu.

"So you'll cool it?" Cody asked. "Like, not a letter every day or anything. Maybe a couple a week. I just don't think it's such a hot idea anymore. So . . . just, you know, taper them off."

"Sure," Zack said soothingly.

"Cool. You're a pal. Well, I'd better hit the waves, right?" Cody picked up his surfboard, nodded a good-bye at Zack, and jogged toward the ocean.

Zack turned and headed back to his car. He never would have thought that Cody could be such a worrywart. He hadn't thought that the guy worried about anything. Cody's strength was his heart, not his mind. Zack had just written another letter to Kelly last night, and even he had to admit he'd surpassed himself. It was so beautiful that even he had felt a little teary eyed. He couldn't slow down now. He was just getting started! Cody would forget his hesitations when Kelly gazed at him with those big blue eyes and told him what a great poet he was.

Meanwhile, Zack had work to do. The job at hand required a little rummaging in his *father's* closet. And he had practicing to do. Tomorrow was the start of the Del Olio Campaign, and preparation was key.

On his way home, Zack stopped by Kelly's house and slipped another love letter into her mailbox.

▲   ▼   ▲

Slater found a parking spot a few blocks from the store. The package was ready when he reached the counter, and the store had a record of his mother's payment. The saleswoman smiled and wished him a good day. Everything had gone like clockwork, but Slater wanted to stamp his feet and scream in frustration.

He'd been angry at Jessie before. As a matter of fact, he'd spent a large portion of the last couple of *years* being angry at Jessie. But that anger had somehow been enjoyable, too. He'd known it would lead to an argument full of quips and wise-cracks, and he'd even grown to like having Jessie slay him with a good insult while her eyes glinted sparks at him. The arguments had become truly enjoyable when they'd started dating, because making up had become vastly more interesting.

Slater could understand that kind of anger. But this was a new experience. He felt a horrible burning sensation in his stomach. He wanted to run hard on the beach or scream his head off or punch a wall. But he knew none of those things would make him feel better. Worst of all, not even seeing *Jessie* would make him feel better. She'd hurt him too much, and she couldn't take that away.

As Slater headed back toward his car, he passed a new restaurant that had opened recently, and his steps slowed. The place had already been featured in several newspapers, and all the reviews said it had terrific food. Slater paused idly to look at the menu. It wasn't too expensive, and from what he could see through the window, the inside looked romantic but not too intimidating. It would be a perfect place to take Jessie for a special evening.

With a stab of pain, Slater remembered that he'd just broken up with her. Sighing, he was just starting to walk away when someone familiar caught his eye. Slater turned back. A tall, attractive man was being led to a table by the hostess. Next to him was a pretty blond woman in a leather skirt and silk blouse. Slater realized with a slow sense of shock that the man was Jessie's father.

Quickly Slater ducked into the shadow of an awning. Maybe Mr. Spano was on a business dinner, he speculated. But something about the woman was familiar. He'd seen a picture of her before. Then he understood. It was Leslie, Mr. Spano's new wife!

Maybe they aren't really together, Slater thought. It could just be an innocent meeting. If they were getting a divorce, like Mr. Spano said, there must be things they had to talk over.

But just then, Leslie reached over and took Mr.

Spano's hand. She leaned across the table, and he leaned across to meet her. They kissed. It wasn't a friendly peck, either. It was definitely a major kiss. A kiss between two people in love.

Slater slowly moved away. It looked like the chances of Mr. and Mrs. Spano getting back together were zilch. Meanwhile, Mr. Spano was leading Jessie and her mother on. He was a double-dealing creep. And the only person who knew the truth was Slater. Now he'd have to break the news to Jessie. And in doing so, he just might break her heart.

▲   ▼   ▲

The next morning, Zack was up and dressed and out of the house before his parents were. He had done his investigative work the day before, talking to Binky Grayson, who just might be his main rival for Dolores's affections. Binky wore a blazer and slacks to school every day, and he claimed not only to have eaten caviar but to have liked it. Dolores actually might be misguided enough to consider him suave.

Binky had let it slip that Dolores liked to walk through the park on the way to school. Zack drove there, parked his car, and hurried over to the exit that would be the most convenient way to Bayside High.

Binoculars around his neck, he ambled down the path and back again, checking his watch. He was beginning to despair when he finally saw Dolores coming toward him, dressed in a silk pantsuit in a deep purple shade.

She smiled in a friendly way as she came up. "Well, hello," she said warmly.

Zack looked surprised, then a bit affronted. He nodded stiffly. "Goot morning," he said. Then he put the binoculars to his eyes and studied the trees.

"We met yesterday," Dolores explained. "I'm Dolores Del Olio. The new transfer student. Remember?"

"Excuse me, ve have not met, madame," Zack said in Rosina's accent. "I vould remember, I am sure."

Now Dolores looked confused. "But I have met you . . . wait a second. You have an accent now."

Zack turned and looked at her. "I have always had an accent," he said. "But I begin to see. You must have met my cousin, Zack Morris, yes?"

Now, Dolores looked even more confused. "Your cousin?"

"He goes to Bayside High. I go to ze Kingston Academy," Zack said, naming a posh private school. "Zack ees ze family cutup, I zink ze phrase is. No?"

Dolores nodded. "So I've heard. And you are?"

Zack clicked his heels. "Rupert Morris at your service, madame."

Dolores flashed a pretty dimple in her left cheek. "You seem very different from your cousin."

Zack leaned over and kissed her hand. "Ah, madame. You haf no idea," he said.

When he straightened, he saw that his plan was already working. Dolores had a definite gleam of interest in her eyes. She took in his silk ascot and blazer as she sidled closer.

"Are you a bird-watcher?" she asked, indicating his binoculars.

"I find eet interesting," Zack said. "Of course, ze birds in Europe are different, so I learn something new every day." He looked into her eyes. "I miss ze leetle birds," he murmured throatily.

"How sad," Dolores said. "Which leetle—I mean, little—bird do you miss the most?"

Zack thought fast. "In my country—"

"Which is?"

"Studovia. It ees small republic near Czechoslovakia, Austria, and, uh, Belgium. My father, ze count, was exiled from the country when I vas a small boy."

"How sad."

"Yes. I remember so vell outside ze palazzo ze puce-throated warbler. Singing his leetle heart out. Such a pretty leetle bird."

"I lived in Europe, too," Dolores said, moving even closer.

"Vere?"

"All over." Dolores gave a deep sigh. "I miss it so!"

"Ah, yes," Zack said. "Monte Carlo, ze Mediterranean, ze South of France!"

"Vienna, Lake Lucerne, Paris!"

"Ze Pyrenees!"

"The Apennines!"

"Ze running of ze bulls!"

"The dancing in the streets!"

Zack took her hand. "You understand, I theenk."

She bowed her head. "I do."

"Ve are both lonely," Zack said, drawing closer.

"Yes," Dolores whispered.

"Miss Del Olio . . . Dolores—" *But wait,* Zack thought. *She's not supposed to fall for Rupert.*

"Yes?" she asked breathlessly.

"I vant you to meet my cousin."

Dolores took a step backward. She sniffed. "But I've already met him, remember?"

"I mean, *really* meet him," Zack said urgently. "You see, Zack ees misunderstood. You must understand, he ees a role model to me."

"Oh, Rupert," Dolores said. "That's funny."

"I do not see what ees funny about it," Zack protested.

Dolores giggled. "Well, Zack Morris is a boy." She took a step closer to him again. She tossed a lock of flaming hair out of her eyes. "You're a man," she cooed.

Uh-oh. It looked like his act was working *too* well. The plan was to get Dolores to think that Zack was the man for her. Even though there was nothing Zack liked better than being on the receiving end of that melting look in Dolores Del Olio's gorgeous topaz eyes, he wanted the receiver to be Zack, not Rupert.

Zack backed away nervously. "Look at ze time. I must get to ze academy. Zey are so strict. But I vill be in the park zees afternoon. Perhaps I vill see you here."

"Perhaps," Dolores said flirtatiously. She waggled her fingers in a wave and headed off down the path. As soon as she was out of sight, Zack ripped off his ascot, shoved the blazer into his pack, and pulled on the cotton sweater he had stowed away. He was awfully glad to get rid of Rupert. The guy was such a phony. Zack was definitely the better man. And the sooner that Dolores realized it, the better.

Chapter 7

Over the next few days, Zack met Dolores in the park every morning and after school. He boned up on polo and race-car driving and European geography, and so far, he hadn't slipped up.

The danger came when Dolores asked him to walk her to school. Zack couldn't refuse, and it was a huge challenge to keep out of sight without being obvious about it. The binoculars helped. Every time he thought he saw someone he knew, he put them to his eyes, swiveled away, and started talking madly about the puce-throated warbler.

The only problem was, his plan wasn't working. Dolores continued to adore Rupert and think Zack was a jerk. No matter how Cousin Rupert praised Zack, she didn't change her mind. She just kept saying how much she admired his family loyalty, even to the black sheep.

"Black sheep," Zack mumbled as he made his way down the hall of Bayside High. "Hah!" At least Kelly was still crazy about him. Of course, she thought she was crazy about *Cody,* but that was only a minor detail. The other day, Cody had asked him to stop writing the letters completely, and Zack supposed he would have to. But first he wanted to deliver a couple of letters he'd already written. They were his finest ever, and he was too proud of them not to give them to her.

Zack wasn't deluded enough to think that he had two girls on the string. But he *did*—sort of. If only they could realize that *he* was the one they were crazy about. It was a dilemma, that was for sure.

Zack was so intent on his dilemma that he almost bumped into Mr. Belding, who was standing outside the home ec room, shaking his head.

"What's the matter, Mr. Belding?" Zack asked. "Did the microwave ovens explode again?"

"No, Zack, it's worse than that," Mr. Belding said with a frown. "Last time it was an accident. Screech didn't mean to explode those burritos. But lately a lot of strange things have been happening on purpose."

"What do you mean?" Zack asked curiously.

"Somebody took all the labels off the cans," Mr. Belding said, indicating the home ec shelves. "Now Mrs. Wozinski doesn't know what's in them. She'll have to open every single can. Probably most of the food will spoil, too."

"It was just a stupid prank," Zack said. "There's the big game coming up with Valley High. You know the school can get pretty crazed."

Mr. Belding shook his head. "This isn't an isolated prank, Zack. Yesterday someone let out all the air in the basketballs in the gym. And the day before, someone switched all the price stickers in the school store. Daisy Tyler bought a notebook for fifteen dollars, and Toby Malone got a pocket calculator for a dollar ninety."

"Whoa," Zack said. "I've got to check this out."

Mr. Belding gave him a severe look. "We changed the prices back again, Zack." Then he frowned. "I'm worried. The thing about pranks is that they can escalate. And sometimes people can get hurt. You don't happen to know anything about these incidents, do you?" Mr. Belding gave him a meaningful look.

Zack held up his right hand. "I swear. I wouldn't do anything like this, Mr. Belding. Even *I'm* not this bad. I wouldn't want to drive Mrs. Wozinski and the coach crazy. I just like driving *you* crazy."

Mr. Belding sighed. "I know. It's not your style. Well, let me know if you hear anything." He ambled off worriedly.

Zack peeked into the home ec room, where Mrs. Wozinski and a student assistant were emptying the cans into plastic containers and labeling them. It looked like the prankster had gotten the results he wanted—teacher and principal aggravation.

And when Mr. Belding was unhappy, Bayside High was unhappy. He mooned around the school with a big worried frown on his face, making everyone else worry, too. There would be a black cloud over Bayside High for weeks unless someone could catch the prankster.

Someone . . .

Someone mature. Someone responsible. Someone clever. Someone with just as devious a mind.

Zack pictured capturing the prankster. It was probably someone huge, like Butch Henderson, the fullback, or someone menacing, like Denny Vane, the class hood. Only this guy would be worse. Zack could just see himself holding the scary guy by the scruff of the neck while Kelly and Dolores gazed at him adoringly. Dolores would realize that Rupert was right—Zack wasn't the troublemaker she thought he was. And Kelly would see that it takes brains, not muscles, to be truly macho.

Of course, the only flaw in the fantasy was that instead of *no* girls, Zack would have two at once. But that was one problem he could definitely handle.

▲   ▼   ▲

Kelly tried to concentrate, but her thoughts flew from the Industrial Revolution straight to the love revolution Cody Durant had caused in her life.

She eased Cody's latest letter out of her notebook and smoothed it into her open textbook. She read over her favorite part again.

There are early mornings at the beach when the fog hasn't lifted yet. Everything is gray and the air is full of mist. And then the sun breaks through. A shaft of light reflects off my board, and diamonds dance on the ocean. That's the only way I can describe how I felt when you came into my life.

Kelly touched the letter with her fingers. Cody was such a special guy. He saw things and felt things in such a deep way. Now that she'd read his letters, she realized that she hadn't really known him at all before.

The only weird thing, Kelly thought with a frown, was that the romance in the letters didn't really spill over into their time together. At first it had, but lately, Cody hadn't been very romantic at all. If she hadn't gotten his letters, she might have thought that he was falling out of love. But that was impossible. His letters told her that.

Maybe something was wrong in his life. He must have a problem that he was afraid to talk to her about. *How sweet of him not to want to burden me*, Kelly thought with a happy sigh. But she had to show him that she wanted to share everything with him—even problems. Now that their love was so deep, he had to know that trust went along with that. Besides, the difference between Cody in his letters and Cody in person was driving her nuts!

"Miss Kapowski?" Mrs. Wentworth frowned at her.

Kelly felt as though she'd been pulled out of a dream. She blinked up at the teacher. "Uh, yes, Mrs. Wentworth?"

"I asked you a question. Describe labor relations during the Industrial Revolution."

"Gee," Kelly said. "All I know is that when my mom was in labor, my dad passed out every time. He has a scar from every single one of my brothers and sisters."

The class rocked with laughter, and Kelly blushed. Mrs. Wentworth glared at her and made a mark in her notebook. Kelly sunk down farther in her chair and hid behind her book. If she didn't straighten things out with Cody soon, she just might flunk out of school completely.

▲   ▼   ▲

"Slater, you can't ignore me forever," Jessie said.

"I'm not ignoring you," Slater said. "I'm avoiding you." He was sitting in a booth at the Max after school. For the past few days, he'd wrestled with his conscience instead of his teammates, and he'd found it a whole lot tougher. He just didn't know what to do. He hated the thought of destroying Jessie's dream.

"Can we talk?" Jessie asked softly.

"I guess we should," Slater said.

Jessie slid gracefully into the booth opposite from him. She clasped her hands on the table and looked down at them. "I'm sorry," she said. "I was wrong the other day. I should have stuck up for you with my dad, no matter what."

Slater let out a relieved breath. "What made you come around?" he asked.

Jessie smiled. "Someone sat me down and showed me the light."

"Kelly?"

She shook her head. "No, not this time."

"Lisa? Zack?" Jessie shook her head again, and Slater threw up his hands. "Oh, no. Don't tell me it was Screech. You'll destroy my faith in the logic of the universe."

Jessie grinned. "It was my dad."

Slater gulped. "Your dad?"

"I was dragging around for days. I mean, I was totally miserable. So finally he asked me what was wrong, and I told him about our fight. He said that he agreed with you completely."

"He did?"

Jessie nodded. "He said that he never meant that I shouldn't see you. He just didn't think you were good enough for me. But he still trusts my instincts, and he admitted that he didn't really get to know you very well. He apologized, Slater. He said he'd leaped to conclusions and it wasn't fair. And he said he still had a lot to learn about being a dad."

"So now you'll see me because your dad says it's okay?" Slater asked in disgust.

Jessie reached out and covered his hand with her own. "No. I'll see you because I love you and I realize that I was an idiot. And I'm asking you to forgive me for being an idiot, and I *won't* point out how many times I've forgiven *you* for being an idiot, because, basically, I'm a nice person."

"For an idiot," Slater added with a grin.

Jessie playfully started to snatch her hand away, but he grabbed it and squeezed it. Her fingers wound around his. "Okay," he said softly. "I forgive you. And I was pretty miserable, too."

"So, you see?" Jessie asked happily. "My dad is a pretty good guy after all."

Slater looked down at their entwined hands. He knew that he shouldn't tell her now. They'd just made up, and he at least would have liked to enjoy the sensation of having Jessie not be mad at him for more than thirty seconds. But that would be taking the easy way out.

"Jessie, I have to tell you something," he said slowly. "I was downtown the other day, and I saw something."

"What?" Jessie asked happily.

"Actually, I saw someone. Your dad. In a restaurant."

"You should have said hello," Jessie said. "You would have seen how nice he can be. He promised me he'd give you a chance."

"It wasn't a good time," Slater said.

"Oh. Was he having a business meeting or something?"

Slater nodded. "Yeah. Or something."

Jessie stiffened slightly. "Slater, what are you getting at?"

"Jessie, he was with Leslie. His wife."

"His *ex*-wife," Jessie corrected hastily.

"They're not divorced yet," Slater pointed out. "They're only separated."

"So?" Jessie said stonily. "Look, so he had lunch with Leslie. They probably had stuff to go over about the divorce."

"So what is she doing in Palisades, Jessie? And they weren't talking about a divorce, I can guarantee it. It looked more like they were talking about a second honeymoon."

Jessie slowly withdrew her hand. "I don't believe you," she said. "Just because you don't like my dad doesn't mean you have to spread rumors about him."

"I'm not," Slater said. "You know I wouldn't do that. I'm just telling you what I saw. Jessie, are you *sure* your father is here to get back with your mother? Because from where I was standing, it sure didn't look like it. It looked like he's going to reconcile with Leslie."

Jessie stood up. "He's not!" she yelled. Her cheeks were flushed, and her eyes were bright. "He's not, okay? You don't know what you're talking about!" She stopped talking for a minute and looked at him. "I have to go. I'll see you later."

For the third time that week, Slater sat alone and contemplated the highs and lows of his relationship with a fiery, temperamental, stubborn, gorgeous creature named Jessie Spano. Were the highs worth the lows? Sure. Balancing on a tightrope was definitely exhilarating. But these days, he was beginning to realize he was working without a net. And the ground below was awfully hard and terribly, terribly cold.

Chapter 8

While Jessie and Slater were talking inside the Max, Kelly had tracked down Cody just outside the door. "Cody," she called, hurrying toward him. "Wait up."

Cody waited. "Hey, Kelly," he said. It wasn't exactly an enthusiastic greeting.

"I hardly saw you at school today," Kelly said. She tried not to sound anxious, but she was. Something was different, and she couldn't tell what. She'd worn her prettiest outfit today, a sky blue miniskirt and flowered top. She'd gotten up early to wash her hair so that it would have extra shine. She'd done everything she could to put that light back into Cody's eyes, but it obviously hadn't worked. He wouldn't even meet her gaze. He was staring over her head at a palm tree.

"What's wrong, Cody?" she asked softly.

"Nothing," he said. "Do you want to get a soda?" He started toward the door of the Max.

"No," Kelly said firmly. She took his arm and led him over to a secluded bench in the Max's small side yard. "Cody, I know something's wrong. Why can't you tell me? Just today you wrote me that you felt you could share anything with me."

Cody looked startled. "Today?"

Kelly nodded. "It was a beautiful letter," she said warmly. "I almost cried in study hall."

"Wait a second. Have you gotten letters this week?"

Kelly nodded, her eyes shining. "Every single day. Each one more precious than the last."

Cody gulped. "And what did I say in today's letter?"

"Don't you remember? 'I feel like your heart beats with mine,'" Kelly quoted. "'I can share anything from a bag of potato chips to my deepest secrets with you.'" She sighed. "That's so true, Cody. I feel the same way. Since I've been getting your letters, I've realized what a deep, caring person you are. I mean, I was crazy about you from the beginning. But now I realize my feelings were mostly infatuation. Now I know the real *you*, Cody," Kelly said in a throbbing voice. "And that's the Cody I love. Kind, warm, sensi—"

"Stop it, Kelly!" Cody put his hands over his

ears and rocked back and forth. "I can't stand it anymore!"

"Stand what?" Kelly asked, alarmed.

"What?" Cody shouted.

"What can't you stand?" Kelly repeated.

"What?" Cody shouted again. "I can't hear you!"

Gently, Kelly removed Cody's hands from his ears. "What can't you stand anymore?" she repeated patiently.

"Kelly, I didn't write those letters," Cody blurted. "I asked a friend to do it. I knew you wanted me to be more romantic, and I'm just not a romantic-type guy. I mean, I'm *cool*, Kelly. I've been trained for it. You don't turn from a cool guy to a mushy guy in a second. So I thought maybe if you got romantic letters, you'd realize how I felt. That's how it was in the beginning, anyway."

Kelly stared at him numbly. She could hardly believe what she was hearing. "You didn't write the letters?" she asked faintly.

Reluctantly, Cody shook his head.

"None of them?"

Cody shook his head again. "Well, I did *sign* one of them."

"You mean you didn't even *read* them?"

He shrugged. "I'm not much of a reader."

Kelly just stared at him. It was like her brain was

on a three-second delay. She couldn't absorb what he was saying. Cody, *her* Cody, wasn't Cody at all! She'd been dreaming about a phantom. She'd been in love with someone else.

"Who?" she demanded suddenly. "Who wrote them?"

Cody looked sheepish. "Gosh, I really can't tell you that, Kelly. It would be, like, a bleach of confidence."

"Breach," Kelly said numbly.

"Breech?" Cody questioned. "No, not him. I don't even know the guy. It wasn't him, I promise you. It was just a buddy helping me out. A favor. Then I asked him to stop, and I guess he didn't."

"You asked him to stop? When?"

"Like a week ago."

"A week ago?" This was getting worse and worse. That was just when Cody started being distant with her. Now Kelly could admit that he *had* been distant. She gave him a keen look. "Why did you ask him to stop?"

Cody looked *really* uncomfortable. "It was just too weird, Kelly. Like, suddenly I was your dream guy because I wrote these letters. But it wasn't me."

"But," Kelly argued, "you said that you *felt* those things. Right?"

"Sure I did."

Kelly thought hard. After all, Rosina had told her that Cody was her true love. Maybe it could still work out. "Well, I guess it wasn't the worst thing in the world," she said slowly. "I mean, it was kind of sweet, actually. And after all, I loved you before I even got the letters. Maybe we can start all over again."

Kelly wasn't sure if she could, but she had felt so much for Cody. She couldn't imagine breaking up with him. He could apologize, and then she could forgive him. Jessie and Slater did it all the time, and they had a practically perfect relationship. Jessie had told her that just the other day.

But Cody's green eyes slid away from hers. He looked down at his feet. "Look, Kelly," he said. "You are a totally gorgeous dish, that is for sure. And you're probably the nicest girl I've ever hung out with. But this has gotten me all confused. It's not exactly a turn-on when your girl likes your letters better than you, if you know what I mean."

"But I *do* like you, Cody," Kelly said, swallowing against a lump in her throat. "I do."

"I'm not a poet, Kelly," Cody said, shrugging. "I'm just a surfer."

"That's fine," Kelly said. "I'm a cheerleader, not Emily Dickinson."

"Kelly, I've met someone else," Cody said.

If Kelly thought she'd been shocked before, now

she was positively floored. Her mouth dropped open. "What?" she croaked.

"I've met someone else," Cody said in a slightly louder tone.

"I *heard* you," Kelly said, annoyed. "I just can't believe it. You said you were in love with me!"

"I was," Cody said. "But I guess my confidence was shot after you got the letters. Anyway, I met someone at the beach, and . . ." His voice trailed off uncomfortably. "I just think we're too young to be tied down," he finished lamely.

"I don't understand," Kelly said, shaking her head.

"Well, you see, Kelly, adolescence is a time of exploration and experimentation," Cody began in an informative tone.

"I *understand* the concept, I just—" Kelly stopped. "Where did you hear that, anyway?"

"From Zack," Cody said. "We're buddies now. He's a solid guy."

Kelly nodded slowly. "I see."

Cody rose. "So no hard feelings?" he asked anxiously.

Kelly looked up. She felt like she'd been kicked in the teeth, but she had her pride. "No hard feelings," she told him.

She sat on the bench and watched as Cody walked away. He was probably heading for the beach and his new girlfriend. Kelly felt a hot spurt of jealousy rise up inside her. Cody would be looking into someone else's eyes. He'd be kissing someone else. He'd be boring someone else with his account of the waves he'd caught that day. He'd be giving someone else pointers on her tan.

"Good riddance," Kelly told Cody's retreating muscular back. But she didn't really mean it. Part of her still loved him. And part of her loved some mysterious writer who claimed to have fifty-three descriptions for the color of her eyes.

She'd give anything to know who it could be. A buddy, Cody had said. Someone with a gift for expression, that was for sure.

Lost in thought, Kelly hardly noticed when Jessie suddenly burst out of the Max. She stalked down the walk, her ponytail flying. Kelly sprang off the bench and ran after her.

"Jessie, hold on!" she said, hurrying up to her friend. When Jessie turned, Kelly saw that she was upset. "What is it? Another fight with Slater?"

"No, it's my *last* fight with Slater," Jessie said grimly. "I've finally come to my senses."

"I just broke up with Cody, too," Kelly said miserably. "Actually, he broke up with me."

Jessie was instantly sympathetic. "That's awful. Are you okay?"

Kelly shrugged. "Sure."

"Me, too," Jessie agreed.

The two friends peeked at each other, then grinned sheepishly.

"I'm crushed," Kelly admitted.

"Flat as a pancake," Jessie agreed gloomily. "You could slip me under a door."

"I was thinking of a window, actually," Kelly said mysteriously. "Do you think you could do me a favor? I really need your help."

"Lead on," Jessie said. "I've got nothing else to do but go to my room and cry."

▲   ▼   ▲

Jessie lived next door to Zack, and they'd been in and out of each other's houses since they'd been kids. When Jessie was ten, Zack had dared her to climb the big oak tree just outside his bedroom window. When she'd been too frightened, he'd teased her unmercifully. That night Jessie had gritted her teeth and climbed the tree all the way up to his window. She'd burst through the window, making Zack yell in fright. That had evened the score, and Jessie had been climbing the tree to Zack's room to say hello ever since.

Kelly had tried the tree route a few times, but Zack's bedroom window could be tricky to open, and she felt more comfortable with Jessie along. With Cody's latest love letter securely in her pocket, Kelly climbed the tree after Jessie, scraping her knees in the process.

"I hope this is worth it," she grumbled.

"Getting the goods on Zack is always worth it," Jessie answered calmly as she swung herself up to a higher branch.

"You're sure he's not home?" Kelly asked worriedly.

"Positive," Jessie said as she reached the thick branch outside Zack's window and gave Kelly a hand up. "He said he had something to do in the park. Maybe he's jogging."

Jessie hit the window frame in a precise spot, then lifted the window up easily. She stepped inside, and Kelly followed. Jessie headed straight for the typewriter on Zack's desk. She rolled a clean sheet of paper into it.

"I feel like Sherlock Holmes," Kelly said nervously.

"I think we're more like Inspector Clouseau," Jessie said.

"At least we didn't fall out of the tree."

"No kidding," Jessie said. "Now read me a couple of sentences."

Kelly took out the letter. " 'Dear Kelly,' " she read, and Jessie responded with a furious pounding on the keys. " 'Have I told you that I have fifty-three descriptions of the color of your eyes? I didn't think that *blue* did them justice.' "

"Oh, brother," Jessie said as she typed.

"I thought it was romantic," Kelly said in a small voice.

Jessie finished typing and ripped the sheet of paper out of the carriage. "Now let's compare," she said.

The two girls bent their heads over the papers. "Look," Kelly said, pointing. "The *R*s are a little faint."

"And the top part of the capital *K* is broken in both of these," Jessie said. They looked at each other.

"He did it," they both said.

Jessie sighed. "Why would we ever doubt it? Whenever there's a scam, Zack is behind it."

Footsteps sounded outside in the hall, and they only had time to stare at each other in horror before the door burst open and Zack came in.

He was unwinding a silk scarf from around his neck, and when he saw the two girls, he jumped backward. "You almost gave me a heart attack!" he cried. "What are you guys doing here?" He stuffed the scarf into his pocket.

"Where were you?" Jessie asked, confused. She took in his blazer and loafers. "A job interview?"

"Never mind that," Kelly said furiously. She shook the two papers at Zack. "I know everything, Zack!"

"You do?" Zack gulped. "Look, I promise I was

going to stop soon. I was! I mean, I'm starting to go bonkers watching those birds every morning."

"What?" Jessie said.

"Don't try to confuse me," Kelly said, taking a step toward him. "I know you wrote those letters for Cody."

Zack's face slowly drained of color. "Oh," he said. "The letters. Kelly, I was just trying to help Cody out."

"He asked you to stop!" Kelly cried. "And you just kept going! If you hadn't done that, I might have figured out that he was losing interest in me. Then I wouldn't have been so surprised when he dumped me!"

"He dumped you?" Zack asked incredulously. "That swine!"

"You're the swine, Zack Morris," Kelly shot back. "It was a cruel, insensitive thing to do. You were probably laughing the whole time. Poor, dumb Kelly will fall for anything, won't she!"

"No, I—"

Kelly tore up the letter and threw the pieces at Zack. Her deep blue eyes were full of tears. "I never thought you could be so mean, Zack," she whispered in a choked voice. "I never thought you could be so cruel. Fifty-three different descriptions of the color of my eyes—give me a break!"

Pushing past him, Kelly ran from the room. Jessie gave him an accusing look and followed.

Zack sat down dazedly on the bed. He shifted uncomfortably, then removed the small binoculars from his rear pocket and tossed them to the floor. He stared at the empty air where Kelly had stood, her eyes full of tears.

"A summer sky," he said aloud. "The first stars at twilight. A robin's egg. A handful of sapphires. A field of cornflowers . . ."

Chapter 9

"Screech, could you pass the catsup?" Jessie asked.

Screech reached over in front of Slater, took the catsup, and sailed it down the table to Jessie.

"Lisa, can you pass the salt?" Slater asked.

Lisa rolled her eyes, but she grabbed the salt from in front of Jessie and passed it to Slater.

"Lisa, would you tell Zack that Coach Neely wants to see him tomorrow morning?" Kelly asked. "He told me to tell him, I don't know why. It's not like Zack and I are *friends* or anything. Friends treat each other honestly and decently. So Zack and I *couldn't* be friends."

Lisa turned to Zack, but he held up a hand. "I heard. You can thank Kelly for me, if you see her."

Jessie spoke up. "Screech, will you tell Zack that

I *won't* be over to help him with his chemistry homework tonight? He'll just have to figure out the periodic table by himself."

"Zack, Jessie isn't coming over tonight," Screech told Zack dutifully.

"Thanks, Screech," Zack said. "I would have been waiting all night."

"Anytime," Screech said, his curly head of hair bobbing.

Lisa suddenly slammed her hand down on the table. "I can't stand this!" she exclaimed. "The Max just isn't the same. Will you guys please make up?"

Kelly and Jessie gave Lisa dirty looks. "Or at least bring your own catsup," Lisa said weakly.

"Some people don't deserve to be forgiven," Kelly said, giving Zack a dark glance.

"That's for sure," Jessie agreed, pointedly not looking at Slater.

"I feel like the whole world is falling apart," Lisa moaned. "All my friends hate each other, there's a school vandal, and the air-conditioning unit is broken at the mall."

"Did you hear the latest about the vandal?" Screech asked. "Today was spaghetti and meatball day—"

"Hey," Slater interrupted, "I didn't get any meatballs with my spaghetti."

"Why should you?" Jessie said in a low tone.

"You already have a meatball for a head."

Screech waved a white napkin in the air. "No firing until I finish my story. The reason there were no meatballs is because someone broke into the kitchen and rolled all the meat into one giant meatball. Then they fried it up in a big skillet."

Lisa giggled. "That's kind of funny."

"It could have been, but they left it in the middle of the floor," Screech went on. "Mrs. Vivandi tripped over it and sprained her ankle when she came in this morning."

"That's terrible," Jessie and Slater said at the same time. They looked at each other, then quickly looked away.

"This is really getting out of control," Lisa said. "Why can't anybody catch this guy? Zack, why don't you try?"

Zack shrugged. "I'm sure the prankster will get caught without my help, Lisa." He didn't want to tip his hand. It would be much better to surprise everyone when he executed another of his brilliant plans and captured the prankster. Zack sneaked a look at Kelly's stony face. *It will take more than a brilliant capture to bring Kelly around,* he thought. *It will take a bulldozer.*

"Besides," Kelly said, "Zack is a champion at *making* mischief, not solving it."

The look she gave him could turn boiling water into ice cubes in ten seconds. *I ought to add Arctic ice to the list of descriptions of Kelly's eyes,* Zack thought. He'd better be on the lookout for that vandal. It might not do him any good with Kelly, but a drowning man would grasp at any tiny straw. And if he couldn't have Kelly, at least he might be able to impress Dolores.

▲   ▼   ▲

After school the next day, Zack was supposed to meet Dolores in the park but not until four-fifteen, so he had a few minutes to wander around the empty halls just in case the prankster was at work.

This would be a good time for him to strike, Zack thought. There were only a few club meetings scheduled, and they were all on the first floor. The second and third floors were completely empty.

Zack prowled the third floor, then the second, then tried the third again. He decided to hit the second one more time. His locker was on that floor, anyway, and he could swing by and pick up his blazer and ascot, then head for the park to meet Dolores.

He walked softly down the halls, peeking into the empty classrooms. Halfway down the hall, he heard a noise. It was a rhythmic squeaking noise, and Zack hoped Screech hadn't let the mice out of the biology lab again. He stopped, listening carefully.

Zack had no idea what the noise was, but he

hurried down the hall, swiftly and silently. He was definitely not alone. Something was going on!

Suddenly he heard a clatter and the noise of running footsteps. Zack started to run. He rounded the corner and stopped. No one was there, but he had kicked a felt-tip marker, which skidded away on the floor and hit the wall. Zack saw several other markers strewn about and realized what the squeaking noise had been. Someone had been writing on poster board.

He looked across the hall. Near the entrance to the balcony of the auditorium was a huge sign that the pep squad had recently put up. It was a picture of the Bayside High mascot, a tiger, eating a raw steak. Big red letters spelled out BAYSIDE HIGH IS REALLY PRIME!

Or, rather, it used to read that. Now the letters had been filled in and marked over, the steak was a puddle of green ooze, and the sign read BAYSIDE HIGH IS REALLY SLIME!

Zack picked up a red felt-tip marker. He had been just moments away from catching the vandal. Next chance, he'd be right on time.

The sound of footsteps came from behind him. Zack whirled around and saw Dolores coming toward him, carrying her books. Her footsteps faltered when she saw him, and she stopped.

"Zack," she said. "Hi." Her eyes widened as she noticed the marker in his hand. Her gaze slowly traveled to the wall, where she noticed the mutilated poster. Then her gaze came back to the marker in his hand again.

"I just found it," Zack said. "It was the strangest thing—"

But Dolores didn't listen. A small squeak escaped her, and she turned and ran back the way she had come, her flats slapping against the floor.

Puzzled, Zack watched her round the corner. Then he looked down at the red marker in his hand and over at the sign.

Groaning, Zack slumped against the wall. You didn't have to be a detective to figure out the evidence. He was at the scene of the crime, and he was holding the weapon. Dolores thought he was the school vandal!

▲   ▼   ▲

When Zack arrived at the park, still trying to tie Rupert's ascot, Dolores was pacing back and forth on the path.

"Oh, Rupert!" Dolores cried, running toward him. She threw herself in his arms. "I'm so glad to see you!"

Zack smelled musky perfume and felt the softness of Dolores's hair against his fingers. He slipped his arms around her and patted her back. He had been scheming to get Dolores in exactly this position for days, but he hadn't wanted it to be for this reason.

"Vat ees it?" he asked. "Ees somethink wrong?"

"I was so frightened," Dolores said, clutching him with anxious fingers. "I thought I was going to faint!"

"Calm down now," Zack said with a nervous chuckle. "I am sure eet can't be zat bad."

"Oh, but it is!" Dolores said earnestly. Her topaz eyes were very wide. "I caught the school vandal! And it's your cousin, Zack!"

"No! Zees cannot be!"

"I'm sorry, Rupert," Dolores said. "But it is. I told you that your cousin was a troublemaker. It's his reputation at Bayside High. He's the one who's been doing all those terrible things at school. I caught him red-handed. Literally!"

"But I am sure you must be mistaken—"

Dolores shook her head. She gripped his shoulders even harder. Zack winced.

"No," she said. "I saw him with a red marker in his hand. He had just finished defacing a sign. There was an evil, guilty look on his face—I'll never forget it." She shuddered. "I thought I was in danger."

"Dolores, Dolores," Zack chided, alarmed. "Do not be silly. Come, sit down." He led her gently to a bench. "Now," he said when they were seated, "let us look at zees. Perhaps Zack had happened by and picked up ze marker. Zen, poof—you theenk he ees ze criminal. That happens all ze time."

"Maybe on TV," Dolores said dubiously.

"But I know my cousin," Zack said desperately. "Zack Morris ees a fine, upstanding citizen. A mature, reliable, uh—all-around great guy, as zey say here. I do not think eet could be him. No, Dolores. You are wrong. Definitely."

Dolores looked at him with shining eyes. "Oh, Rupert," she said. "Your loyalty is so impressive."

"It ees not loyalty," Zack said quickly, almost losing his accent in his excitement. "It ees just knowledge of my cousin's character. He ees not capable of thees kind of thing."

Dolores only sighed. "Rupert," she said, patting his arm, "you're just so wonderful."

Zack gave up. He saw there was no way he could convince her. "Dolores, you must promise me somethink," he said. "Say nothink. I vill talk to my cousin." He smiled. "You vill promise me zees?"

She nodded. "If you want me to, Rupert."

"I think eet is better this way. No?"

"I guess so."

Zack smiled at her uneasily. He'd really gotten himself into a mess now. It was all Rupert's fault, he thought, annoyed. He'd have to give that continental crank a talking-to.

▲   ▼   ▲

"This has gone far enough," Slater said to Jessie. "You're coming with me."

Jessie tilted her head back and put her hands on her hips. "Who's going to make me?" she demanded.

Slater didn't answer. Instead, he picked her up in his arms and carried her, protesting angrily, to his big old Chevy.

"Slater, put me down!" Jessie yelled. "You can't do this!"

Slater dumped her into the front seat. "I just did, momma."

Jessie glared at him through the front windshield as he made his way to the driver's seat. She was furious, but she didn't slide out and stalk away. Part of her was glad Slater had finally forced her to talk to him again. But part of her was still angry.

Slater drove through the streets of Palisades in silence. If he wasn't going to talk, she wouldn't, either. Jessie crossed her arms and stared out the window.

She thought he'd drive to the beach, their favorite place to talk, but instead, Slater drove downtown. Jessie was longing to ask where they were going, but she took one look at Slater's set face and clamped her mouth shut.

Finally Slater eased the car into a parking spot on a downtown street. Jessie couldn't stand it any longer.

"May I ask where we're going?" she asked in an icy tone.

"You can ask," Slater said. "But I won't tell you."

He got out of the car, crossed to the passenger side, and hauled her out. He kept her hand securely in his as he led her down the street to an elegant café. Jessie felt her heart soften. He was going to treat her to a nice meal out! That was such a sweet way to apologize for being such a complete and utter slime ball. It was just like Slater.

But that didn't mean she had to melt immediately. Jessie was silent and stiff as the hostess led them to a table by the window. Slater shook his head and pointed to another table in the corner. A large palm stood near it, shielding it from the rest of the diners. It was completely private and very romantic.

Jessie slid into the chair. "This is nice," she said grudgingly.

"Yeah," Slater said. He picked up his menu, but he didn't look at it. He drummed on the table nervously and looked around at the other diners.

Jessie opened the menu and studied the list of choices. Everything looked delicious. She was deciding between a spinach salad with strips of spicy chicken breast and a little pizza with roasted peppers when Slater put his hand on her arm.

"So," Jessie said. "You finally want to apolo—"

"Shhh," Slater said. He put his finger to his lips. Then he pointed through the leaves of the palm.

Giving him a puzzled look, Jessie leaned forward and looked through the leaves. She gasped when she saw her father threading through the tables. Then she felt sick. On his arm was a blond and smiling Leslie. As Jessie watched in horror, her father leaned over and kissed Leslie gently on the lips.

Jessie looked at Slater. "You see?" he said softly. His soft brown eyes were full of sorrow. "I didn't lie."

Slowly Jessie lifted her napkin from her lap. She spent a long time folding it in precise creases, running a thumbnail along them. Then she placed it back on her plate. Finally she looked up at Slater with bleak eyes.

"No," she said quietly. "You showed me that you didn't. Are you happy now, Slater?"

Then she rose and walked out of the restaurant, her head held high. Her father had his back to her and was ordering a bottle of wine, so he didn't see her at all.

Chapter 10

That night Kelly checked on her littlest brother, Billy. He was sleeping peacefully, his little hand curled up into a fist. Her brother Kyle was doing his homework, Kerry and Erin were watching TV, and Nicki, her fifteen-year-old sister, was in her room. Recently Nicki had renounced being a tomboy and had embraced being a girl, and now she spent her nights studiously trying on makeup and clothes.

Mr. and Mrs. Kapowski were out at a movie, and Kelly was in charge. Normally it was a dubious honor, but tonight Kelly was glad of the responsibility. It was a relief to have her brothers and sisters to worry about. She didn't have to think about her own problems.

The only problem was that nobody needed her tonight, and there was nothing to do. Nobody was fighting, Billy wasn't crying, and the dishes were done. There was nothing to do but go to her room and finally do what she had been putting off all evening long.

Kelly closed the door and slipped the package of letters out from underneath her pillow. She sat cross-legged on the bed, untied the lilac ribbon, and sat for a moment with the letters in her lap. Then, with a deep sigh, she slipped out the first letter and began to read.

For the next hour, Kelly sat and read and reread every single letter. For the first time, she read the words without thinking about Cody. This time she thought about who really had written them.

When she finally had finished, she sat quietly, staring at the letters in her lap. The beautiful words still flitted in her head like butterflies. Could Zack really have written these? How could she know him so long and so well . . . and not know him at all?

Kelly went over the letters in her mind. She thought not so much of his words of love but of Zack's descriptions of what he thought and felt. And even though she was still angry at him, she had to admit to herself that sincerity rang through every line.

Zack hadn't written these letters just as a favor to Cody. They were too meaningful, too special. She had loved them for real reasons. They weren't glib or insincere. She had fallen in love with the writer because of that.

Kelly slowly gathered up the letters and tied them in a bundle again. Yesterday she had almost ripped every one of them to shreds, and now she was glad she hadn't. Maybe, just maybe, they were whispering a message to her that she shouldn't ignore.

Could Zack have written those letters if he didn't still care? And if he *did* still care, did he know it? How could he have written them if he *did*? He had written the words of love that were supposed to deliver her straight to Cody Durant.

Kelly sighed and flopped back on the bed. She fingered the lilac ribbon. There were so many tantalizing questions! Maybe it was time she found out the answers.

▲   ▼   ▲

Slater left three messages at Jessie's with her mother, but Jessie never called back. At school she pulled her disappearing act again. Finally he cornered her by her locker at the end of the day.

"Look," he said awkwardly. "I'm sorry about yesterday. Really sorry. I should have warned you, I guess. But I knew you wouldn't stay."

"You're right," Jessie said tonelessly. "I probably wouldn't have."

Slater moved closer and tried to touch her arm, but Jessie pulled away. "What I can't figure out," Jessie said, "is why you'd want to hurt me like that."

"I don't want to hurt you!" Slater exclaimed in frustration. "I want to help you face reality!"

Jessie bit her lip. "Look, Slater. Maybe that's true. And you're right—I have to sort some things out. I really need some time to myself."

He stared at her for a long second. He couldn't believe this was happening again. "You won't let me help you?" he said. Jessie stared at him mutely, her delicate skin flushed. Slater felt as though he'd been kicked in the stomach. "Okay," he said finally. "If that's what you want. No problem."

Jessie sighed. "Oh, Slater," she murmured. "I'm so tired of fighting with you."

"I know what you mean," Slater responded tightly. They stared at each other for a moment, then looked away.

"I guess there's nothing more to say," Jessie said finally.

Slater nodded stiffly. "Guess not."

"Do you want to go to the Max?" Jessie asked. "I told Lisa I'd meet her there."

"Why not?" Slater said tersely.

They walked in silence to the Max. There was such a mixture of anger and sadness in how they felt that neither one of them could say anything at all. Words had become time bombs, and neither one of them would risk blowing everything completely to bits.

With relief, Jessie saw Lisa's smiling face at the Max. Screech and Kelly were there, too. With all their friends around them, she and Slater wouldn't have to talk at all.

Lisa was talking about the school vandal as Slater and Jessie sat down. "Everyone was waiting to see what he'd do today," she said, twirling a straw in her soda. "I mean, defacing the poster was small change. I thought for sure we'd see something more amazing."

"I'm glad we didn't," Screech said. "I had a nightmare about the giant meatball. I dreamed that Mrs. Vivandi made me eat the whole thing."

Everyone laughed. "You'd need a really huge Alka-Seltzer for that," Slater observed.

"Today was Deli Day in the cafeteria," Screech said. "I'm really glad I won't dream about giant knishes tonight."

"This guy is getting out of hand," Slater remarked. "The football team is completely spooked. Everyone is afraid the prankster is going to do something drastic on Saturday during the big game."

"This is awful," Kelly said. "We've just got to beat Valley High!"

"We have to do something," Lisa declared. "I have a new dress for the Victory Dance, and I don't want anything to spoil it."

"So let's catch the vandal," Slater proposed. "I have a theory."

"Great," Kelly said. "What is it, Slater?"

"I think I know where the vandal is going to strike next," Slater said, leaning over the table and lowering his voice. "The prop room. It makes sense. What better way to strike than to mess with the decorations for the rally and the big game?"

"I bet you're right, Slater," Lisa said, nodding. "That's the logical place to strike next."

"So what should we do?" Kelly asked.

"Stake it out," Slater said with a shrug. "After school on Friday, everyone always clears out of school. I bet that's when the prankster will appear."

"Count me in," Kelly said.

"Me, too," Lisa declared.

Everyone looked at Jessie. "Count me in, too," she said with a shrug.

Everyone looked at Screech. "I'd say count me in, too," he said, "but I've lost count."

"Where's Zack?" Slater asked. "He'll want to be in on this."

"He's never around lately," Jessie said.

"I've hardly seen him," Lisa said.

"I tried to track him down after school," Kelly said. "I really need to talk to him."

"He's been superbusy," Screech said with an air of authority. "He told me all about it."

"What do you mean, Screech?" Kelly queried. "What's he been doing?"

Screech went blank. "I don't know what he's doing. He just told me all about how busy he was. He didn't say with what."

"Thanks, Screech. That's a big help," Slater said.

Dolores Del Olio approached their table hesitantly. "Hi," she said softly. "Would you guys mind if I sat down for a minute?"

"Sure, Dolores," Slater said in a friendly way. He moved over so that Dolores could sit next to him. Jessie frowned but quickly turned it into a welcoming smile when Slater looked at her.

"Hi," Jessie said. "I'm Jessie Spano."

Everyone else introduced themselves, and Dolores nodded at all of them. "I've seen you guys around," she said shyly. "You seem really nice, and I know I can trust you."

"Of course you can, Dolores," Slater said. "What's the problem?"

"Well," Dolores said, "I saw something the other day. Someone was . . . doing something bad. I don't want to go to the principal and get this person in trouble. So I thought if I just went to this person's friends, they could get this person to stop doing it. Do you know what I mean?"

The gang exchanged glances. "I think so," Kelly said. "But it would help if you could tell us who the person is and what they've done."

"Okay." Dolores took a deep breath. "I saw the school vandal," she said in a hushed tone.

Everyone leaned closer to Dolores. "Who is it?" Kelly breathed.

"It's Zack Morris," Dolores said.

Everyone gasped. Then they exchanged shocked glances.

"No way," Lisa said.

"It can't be," Kelly protested.

"I don't believe it," Jessie scoffed.

"Even *I* don't believe it," Slater declared.

Screech only gulped. "I'm speechless," he said. "I know I'm talking right now, but I am."

"It's true," Dolores insisted. "I caught him red-handed. He was defacing that sign yesterday. You know, 'Bayside High Is Really Slime.' "

"It just can't be Zack," Kelly said.

Dolores looked puzzled. "I don't understand why you guys are so surprised. I thought Zack was a real troublemaker."

"Well, he is," Kelly admitted. "But he's not *that* kind of troublemaker. He might have a scam that gets out of hand, but he never deliberately sets out to destroy something."

"He's kind of hard to explain," Jessie said.

Dolores stood up. "Well, I just wanted to tell you. I'm not going to go to Mr. Belding or anything. But Zack just has to stop."

"We'll tell him, Dolores," Lisa promised.

Dolores nodded and walked away. There was a long silence at the table.

"Zack *has* been acting weird lately," Jessie said hesitantly.

"Every time you ask him where he's going after school, he won't give you a straight answer," Slater said.

"He just did something to me that I'd never have imagined in a million years," Kelly admitted softly.

"Well, even if he *is* acting weird, he's certainly dressing better," Lisa put in. "I saw him wearing the prettiest silk scarf around his neck yesterday after school. I asked him where he got it, but he practically ran away."

"So who's going to tell him that we know?" Slater asked gloomily.

"We *don't* know," Jessie pointed out quickly. "Dolores could be wrong."

"But she said she caught him red-handed," Kelly said. "It's so strange."

Suddenly Screech stood up. His face was red, and his hands were clenched. "I can't believe you people. You think he's guilty!"

"No, we don't, Screech," Kelly told him. "We're just . . . wondering."

"Maybe Zack is having personal problems that we don't know about," Jessie said doubtfully.

"Look, Screech," Slater said. "We won't say anything to Zack, but we'll follow through on our plan to stake out the prop room. That way, if he's guilty, at least we'll be the people who catch him."

"He won't be there," Screech insisted.

Slater shrugged. "Okay, he won't. But then we'll know."

"You'll all see," Screech said. "You'll see that he's innocent." He turned and ran out of the Max, his purple-striped shirt streaming behind him.

▲   ▼   ▲

Sunk in gloom, Screech ignored the bus and walked all the way home from the Max. He just couldn't believe that Zack was the culprit. Zack was his buddy. He looked up to him. How could he be the giant meatball maker? Knowing Zack, if he *had* done it, he would have confessed as soon as he found out about Mrs. Vivandi's sprained ankle.

As Screech turned the corner onto his block, he saw a group of boys sitting on a front lawn. It was his neighbor, Andy Noland, and his best friends Sandy and Bobby, also known as Bobo. All three were freshmen at Bayside High. They were definitely geeks, and Screech knew they looked up to him as the ultimate, cool older man.

"Hi, guys," he greeted them as he walked by.

"Hey, Screech," Andy said. "Have you seen that weird guy hanging around school lately?"

Screech stopped. "What weird guy?"

"Bobo talked to him one day," Andy said. "And Sandy saw him."

"He was way at the end of the block near school," Sandy said. "And I saw him in the park, too. He had binoculars."

"He was a totally weird guy," Bobo said. "He had a weird accent. He said his name was something weird—oh, Rupert. A real weirdo. It was like, really, I don't know—"

"Weird?" Screech supplied.

Bobo nodded solemnly. "Exactly. He looked familiar, too."

"You keep saying that, Bobo," Andy said in exasperation. "I wish you'd remember who he looked like."

"I know what Bobo means, though," Sandy said. "I think he looked like Rex Harrison."

"Who's Rex Harrison?" Andy asked.

"You know, the British guy," Sandy said. "The actor. He was in whatchamacallit, that old movie, you know, where he teaches the girl how to talk right? It's a musical. Or maybe I'm thinking of Laurence Olivier."

"Who?" Bobo said.

"The only British guy I know is Queen Elizabeth," Andy said.

Screech cleared his throat. "When did you first see the weird guy?"

Bobo and Sandy looked at each other. "A couple of weeks ago, I think," Bobo said, and Sandy nodded. "Or maybe the beginning of this week." Sandy nodded again.

"Very interesting," Screech murmured. He turned back to the boys. "Now, look, I don't want you guys to worry. I'll keep an eye out, okay? If this guy is trouble, he'll have to deal with Samuel E. Powers first." Screech hurried away, his long, skinny legs propelling him home.

He closed the door to his house with an exultant bang. This was some piece of news! This stranger had shown up right when the pranks began. And even Bobo had said he was weird. This guy Rupert must be the culprit!

Screech bounded upstairs to his room to get his Sherlock Holmes hat. The game was afoot, and he knew exactly how to trap the master criminal. He would catch Rupert and clear Zack's name for good!

Chapter 11

That evening Jessie told her mother that she was going to the city library to research a term paper. But instead she drove north along the beach road until she got to the Palisades Beach Resort Hotel.

Jessie turned into the curving drive of the hotel. The long, low stucco building was glowing faintly pink in the sunset. Palm trees waved around it, and the lush green lawn was like a soft carpet leading up to the front door.

Jessie parked the car and walked inside to the lobby. She headed straight for the big staircase and started up. She already knew her father's suite number—207—from calling him that week. The room was all the way at the end of the second-floor corridor. Jessie hesitated only a minute, then knocked sharply.

In only a few seconds, the door opened, and Leslie stood there, staring at her. "Jessie," she said.

"Very good, Leslie," Jessie said crisply.

Concern crossed Leslie's face. "I was just surprised, that's all. Come on in." She led the way into the spacious living room of the suite. "Alex," she called. "I think you'd better come out."

"I'm on the phone," he called.

"I think you'd better hang up," Leslie called back, her eyes on Jessie's face.

"What is it, sweet—" Jessie's father stopped as he walked into the room and saw Jessie. "I was just on the phone with your mother," he told her. He walked toward her and kissed her cheek. Jessie stood stiffly, not responding.

"I didn't expect to see you tonight," Mr. Spano said.

"I'll bet," Jessie said. Her eyes flicked over at Leslie.

Leslie bent over and picked up her purse. "I think I'll go get a cup of coffee," she said softly.

The door closed behind her, and Jessie and her father stared at each other. "Will you sit down, pumpkin?" he asked gently.

Jessie flinched. "Don't call me that," she said. But she let him lead her to one of the soft apricot couches by the fireplace.

"Your mother called because she was worried about you," her father said. "She says you've been pretty depressed this past week. At first she thought it was because of an argument with Slater. But she's been going over in her mind some things you've said lately, and she thinks you might be hoping that we'll get back together. Is that true, Jessie?"

Jessie looked at the fire. She wasn't ignoring her father; she just couldn't answer him because a lump the size of a basketball was in her throat. She shrugged.

"If I gave you that impression, I'm sorry," her father said seriously. "I never thought that after all these years, you'd still be hoping."

Jessie found her voice. "But, Daddy, you said you were separated from Leslie," she said. "And you and Mom seemed so happy to be with each other."

Her father clasped his hands and looked down at them. "I *was* separated from Leslie," he said slowly. "She left me. And your mother and I were happy to be with each other. It's the first time since the divorce that we've really been able to talk. That's because of Leslie."

"What do you mean, Daddy?" Jessie asked, confused. "You just said that Leslie left you."

Her father sighed. "When Leslie left, she made the same charges against me your mother did ten years ago. It absolutely shocked me, Jessie. Was I going to blow another marriage? Hadn't I learned anything from the first one? So when this deal came up with the Palisades Beach Resort Hotel, I jumped at it. I wanted to come back and talk to your mom. Or rather, I wanted to listen to her. *Really* listen. And I'm ashamed to say that it just might have been for the very first time."

Jessie didn't say anything. She could hear the pain in her father's voice. And she couldn't believe the pain was from that blond twit, Leslie. He must really love her!

Her father reached over and took her hand. "I've learned some hard lessons this week," he said. "Your mother helped me. And because she did, Leslie came back to me. She flew down two days ago and we've been talking ever since. I think we're going to make it. She's a special woman, Jessie. I wish you'd give her a chance."

"She's just an interior decorator," Jessie said with scorn. "I don't think we have much in common." She knew the words were harsh and unfair, but she was so angry that she couldn't control them.

Her father didn't pull away or get angry, the way she thought he would. "Do you know that Leslie has a master's degree in English literature?" he asked. "Do you know that she started a coalition of designers and architects in San Francisco who reclaim and renovate houses for the homeless? Do you know that when she was sixteen she was in a car accident and was told that she'd never walk again?"

"No," Jessie whispered. She hadn't known any of those things.

"I wish you'd get to know her, Jess," her father said. "Do you have so little respect for me that you'd think I'd pick a bimbo to spend the rest of my life with?"

Suddenly Jessie burst into tears. It was hearing the words *spend the rest of my life with*. For the first time, she really faced the fact that her father wasn't coming back. She cried and cried and just couldn't stop. Her father held her until the tears slowed and she started to hiccup.

Finally Jessie pulled away. There was a dark splotch on her father's suit from her tears. "I hope this hotel has valet service," she said, sniffing. "Your suit is a mess."

Mr. Spano laughed. When he stopped, he touched her cheek tenderly. "I'm so sorry I hurt you, pumpkin," he said. "I seem to have bungled everything. I know how hard it was for you when I left—you were only seven years old. Your mother and I were just no good together, and it was starting to affect you. So much anger in the house wasn't good. I can't give those years back to you, and I can't make up for them. The only thing I can do is be there for you now, as much as I can."

Jessie looked into the fireplace. "I wanted to be a family so much," she whispered.

"I know," her father said gently. "And it breaks my heart that it's the only thing I can't give you.

But next year, you'll be going to college. You'll become more independent, and you'll start to make your own life. I hope you'll always let me be part of it."

"Of course you'll always be in my life, Daddy," Jessie said, turning back to him. "I love you."

"And I love you," her father answered. "I think this deal is going through, so I'll be in Palisades pretty often from now on."

With tears in her eyes, Jessie nodded. "That'll be great," she told him.

He reached out and tucked a lock of hair behind her ear. "Honey, we're still a family," he said. "All of us. We're just not a very conventional one."

Jessie smiled through her tears. "Well, that ought to suit me," she said, smiling. "Since when have I ever liked anything to be conventional?"

"Now, that sounds like the daughter I know," her father said with a laugh, and he enveloped her in a big, satisfying hug.

▲   ▼   ▲

The next day at school, Screech arrived early. He hurried to the main bulletin board in the front hall, where students put up notices to sell skateboards or catcher's mitts, offer typing services, or even leave messages for each other. Everybody usually checked the board once a day to see if anything funny or unusual was there.

Screech looked around carefully, then quickly pulled a piece of paper out of his pocket and tacked it to the board. He read it over once, just to be sure that it was perfectly worded.

RUPERT, MY MYSTERY MAN, COME TO ME. I'M READY FOR YOUR LOVE. THE PROP ROOM, FOUR P.M.

"That should do it!" Screech murmured. "By four-thirty, Zack will be a free man." Then he dashed away.

▲   ▼   ▲

Zack saw the notice on the bulletin board on the way to English class. He did a double take and looked closer. A note for Rupert! It couldn't be. But there it was. *Rupert, my mystery man*—it had to be Dolores. Just this morning in the park, she had said that she knew so little about him. Apart from the fact that he loved to play polo and always stayed at the Ritz in Paris, of course.

She probably figured that Zack would tell his cousin about the note. Under normal circumstances, Zack would be thrilled that the luscious Dolores was ready for Rupert's love. But lately he'd begun to realize that Rupert wasn't ready for hers. And neither was Zack.

It wasn't that Dolores wasn't gorgeous, or sweet, or fun to be with. She was all of those things. It was that Zack still had Kelly on his mind. Even though he knew that he'd hurt her and blown his chances with her by writing the letters for Cody, he still couldn't get up steam to really pursue Dolores. It just wasn't fun anymore.

Zack took the card off the bulletin board and crumpled it. He'd have to go, of course. But he'd only meet Dolores to tell her good-bye. Studovia had undergone a complete revolution and had invited the aristocracy back. It was time for Rupert to say bon voyage.

▲   ▼   ▲

"Okay," Screech said. "Let's synchronize our watches. I have three fifty-three."

"I don't have a watch," Lisa complained.

"Okay," Screech fretted. "I'll have to lend you mine."

"Then how will you know what time it is?" Kelly asked.

"I won't be able to see the time, anyway," Screech said. "I'll be in the tiger, and it'll be too dark." He pointed to the large stuffed tiger that was in the middle of the room. Earlier Kelly and Jessie had removed the stuffing. Screech planned to crawl inside it—for a perfect hiding place.

"Then why are we synchronizing our watches?" Jessie asked.

"Because that's what Sherlock Holmes would do," Screech answered logically. He pointed to his hat.

Lisa rolled her eyes. "Just be glad he didn't bring the pipe, too," she murmured to Jessie.

"Enough!" Slater exploded in exasperation. "We don't have to know what time it is. We just have to pop out when the prankster comes in. Kelly, you get behind those costumes. Lisa, you can fit underneath that tarp."

"Ewww," Lisa said. "I'll get all dusty."

"We all have to make sacrifices," Slater told her sternly. "Jessie, you come with me. Everybody, hurry up!"

Slater grabbed Jessie's wrist and pulled her to the utility closet. He shoved her inside, then followed her. His foot hit a pail, and it clanged.

"Shhhh," Jessie whispered.

Slater gave her a dirty look and tried to squeeze inside the closet. It was an awfully close fit.

"Ow," Jessie murmured. "Your elbow is in my side."

"Sorry."

"Now you're pulling my hair."

"Sorry. There." Slater rearranged himself. "Is that better?"

Jessie nodded. Slater was right against her, toe to toe, eye to eye. She could feel the skin of his arm against hers, his knees bumping her knees. "It's fine," she whispered weakly.

"Fine." Slater swallowed. Jessie was so close. *And for once, she'll have to keep her mouth shut,* he thought.

Jessie tried to lean back, but there was nowhere to go. Slater was looking at her intently with soft, dark eyes. *At least he isn't allowed to talk,* she thought.

"I think we'll fit better," Slater whispered, "if you could just move your head a little tiny bit—"

"Shhhh," Jessie said.

She moved her chin up a millimeter. He moved his head down a millimeter. Their lips met.

"I—" Jessie started.

"Shhhh," Slater urged. "No talking," he whispered. Then his soft mouth descended on hers again.

▲   ▼   ▲

Zack checked his watch. Four o'clock. Right on time. He adjusted his ascot and smoothed his hair flat into the conservative Rupert style. He was glad that the school was so empty. It would be impossible to explain this stupid ascot to anyone he knew, especially the gang.

Slowly Zack pushed open the creaky prop-room

door, then closed it behind him. There were no lights on, and the dusky shadows were a little unnerving. If Dolores was trying to set a romantic mood, she wasn't succeeding. The place looked like a haunted house, not a love nest. Even the Bayside High tiger looked ominous, crouched in the middle of the floor.

Zack inched farther into the room. This was positively eerie. He peered into the dark shadows. "Come out, come out, wherever you are," he whispered softly.

Just then Zack thought he saw something move. He turned and saw the tiger lurching menacingly toward him. Zack let out a piercing yell.

Then the tiger spoke. "Zack, shhhh. It's only me."

Zack sat down heavily on a dusty tarp. A thin scream came from underneath it. *What's going on?* Zack wondered crazily. Something underneath the tarp was pushing at him.

"Get off me!" the tarp said.

Zack fell off the tarp onto the floor. Lisa poked her head out. "You crushed me," she wailed. "And besides that, you wrinkled my skirt."

Screech crawled out of the tiger. "Lisa, are you okay? Unhand her, you cad."

"I'm not handing her!" Zack protested. He rubbed his head confusedly. "Would someone please tell me what's going on?"

Kelly stepped out from behind a rack of costumes from the Bayside High Players. Even in the gloom, he could see the accusation in her eyes. "Oh, Zack," she said. "How could you?"

"I didn't know Lisa was underneath it," Zack said, pointing to the tarp. "I promise."

Kelly shook her head. "You know what I mean. You're the Bayside High prankster!"

Chapter 12

Just then Screech turned on the lights. They blazed in Zack's face, and he blinked up at his three interrogators.

"You've got to be kidding," he said.

Kelly put her hand on his arm and pulled him to his feet. "Don't bother to deny it, Zack. We know it's true. We just caught you, and besides, Dolores Del Olio saw you deface that sign."

"What I want to know is how you made that meatball," Screech said. "Wow."

"We won't tell anyone about this, Zack," Lisa promised. "But why did you do it?"

Zack looked from one face to another. "I can't believe you guys think it was me. How could you think that I did those stupid things?"

"Well, you *are* wearing an ascot, Zack," Screech pointed out. "That's pretty stupid."

Zack ripped off the ascot and shoved it into his pocket. "I'm not the prankster," he snarled.

"If you're not, then what were you doing here in the dark?" Kelly asked pointedly.

Zack hesitated. He couldn't tell Kelly about Rupert and Dolores. Then she'd *never* forgive him.

Kelly hung her head sadly. "You see?" she said.

Lisa shook her head. "Oh, Zack."

Zack turned to Screech. "Even you, Screech?" he asked.

"I didn't believe it," Screech said. "I stuck up for you. We all had this plan to trap the real prankster."

"Speaking of 'we,' " Lisa said. "Where are Jessie and Slater?"

"I guess they can't hear us," Kelly said. She went over to the closet and yanked open the door. Jessie and Slater were locked in a torrid embrace.

Lisa giggled. "Some detectives."

Slater and Jessie sprang out of their lip lock. "What's going on?" Slater said.

"We caught the prankster," Lisa told them, indicating Zack.

"I'm not—" Zack started.

But suddenly they heard a noise. Someone was heading toward the prop room. Quickly Kelly sprang for the lights and shut them off. Within seconds she was back behind the rack of costumes, Slater and Jessie were back in the closet, Lisa was underneath the tarp, and Screech had crawled underneath the unstuffed tiger. At the last moment, Zack jumped behind the rack with Kelly.

The door creaked open, then closed. A dark figure moved into the room. Slowly the figure walked toward the game decorations and pep rally favors in the corner.

Zack sprang out and grabbed the intruder by the elbow. The figure tried to twist away, but he held on fast. "Somebody turn on the lights!" he called.

The lights blazed on, and Zack found himself looking into the seductive face of Dolores Del Olio. But now the lovely Dolores only looked frightened.

"Let go of me!" she said fearfully.

Zack dropped her arm and then remembered the note. Of course. Dolores was only here to meet Rupert.

"Rupert's not here, Dolores," he said in a low tone. "I saw your note on the board."

But Kelly heard him. "Who's Rupert?" she asked.

"She didn't come here to meet Rupert," Screech said. "*I* wrote that note. Besides, look."

Screech pointed to Dolores's other hand. She was holding a can of spray paint.

"Holy cow," Zack said. "You *are* the prankster!"

Dolores shrank back against the wall. "Uh-oh," she said weakly.

"Dolores," Jessie said wonderingly. "It was you all along?"

"How could you have accused Zack?" Kelly demanded angrily.

A tear slowly slipped down Dolores's pretty cheek. "I'm so sorry," she said in a choked voice. "This was going to be my last prank, I promise."

"But why did you do the other ones at all?" Zack asked.

Dolores sighed. "I've gone to a different school for every year of high school. You guys don't know what that's like."

"I do," Slater said.

Dolores turned to him. "That's right. You traveled around because your dad was in the army. Then maybe you know how I feel. I never get to make friends. As soon as people warm up to me, I'm gone."

"I guess it didn't help being in a bunch of foreign countries, either," Slater said grudgingly. "I know how that is, too."

Dolores looked down. "Actually, that's not, uh, strictly true. I haven't lived in Italy, France, Austria, England, or Luxembourg."

"Where, then?" Lisa asked.

Dolores gulped. "Indiana, Illinois, Connecticut, Virginia, New Mexico, and here. I mean, there were other states, but those are the highlights."

"That's quite a difference," Jessie pointed out dryly. "Indiana is a long way from Paris."

"My dad is a troubleshooter for companies that

are having problems," Dolores explained. "I was born in Gary, Indiana, and I've been moving around ever since."

"That does sound tough," Lisa said, sympathy creeping into her voice.

"This was my last shot," Dolores said. "Usually I just creep into a new school and nobody notices me. Nobody sits with me in the cafeteria and nobody walks with me to class. Then finally, maybe one nice person befriends me. If I'm lucky. Even if I have nothing in common with that person, it's a big relief to have someone to talk to, so I end up acting like their best friend. I just couldn't face another year like all those others. Especially my senior year."

"So what did you do?" Slater asked. "Decide to be a criminal instead of a wallflower?"

"Not exactly," Dolores said. "You see, I was so miserable that my mom took charge. She took me to this great place in L.A. and I got a makeover. She bought me a whole new wardrobe. She said I could make a difference this time. But I was scared," Dolores said haltingly. "I didn't want to disappoint her. Even though I hated being a wallflower, at least it was safe. I didn't know if I *could* make real friends or join a popular crowd. So I came up with this plan."

Dolores hesitated. "Go on," Zack urged, his arms crossed. Everyone else seemed to be melting from

Dolores's story, but he wasn't. After all, he was the one she was trying to get into trouble.

"Well, I noticed from going to lots of different schools that there's usually a pattern. In one of the cool groups, there's always a guy who's a troublemaker, a wise guy. So I thought if there was a bunch of pranks and everyone thought this certain guy did them and I shielded him, his friends would be supergrateful and would want to be friends with me. So I picked you," she said, turning to Zack. "I'm really sorry. But I figured since you'd done so many other bad things, it wouldn't hurt to have just one more thing pinned on you. And nobody else would know but your friends, anyway."

Jessie nodded slowly. "Actually, it's sort of logical," she said.

"It makes sense," Slater agreed.

"Easy for you guys to say," Zack grumbled. "It's not you she was throwing mud at."

"Zack, I really am sorry," Dolores said again. "Rupert tried to tell me you were a great guy. I guess I just didn't want to believe it."

"Who's Rupert?" Kelly asked again.

"What I don't understand, Dolores," Zack said quickly, "is why you had to invent that exotic background for yourself."

She shrugged. "I guess that was the part of the plan that went a little overboard."

"The *part*?" Zack asked incredulously. "I'd say it was the whole thing."

"I just thought everybody would be more impressed if I had an exciting background," she said. "It was dumb. The only one who was impressed was Rupert, but he's a real snob."

"Who's Rupert?" Kelly asked a third time.

"Well," Zack said quickly, "I'm glad you learned your lesson, Dolores. We all forgive you, don't we, guys? And *I* forgive all my friends for thinking I was the prankster. Someday I'll get over the hurt, I'm sure." Zack swiped at the part of his cheek where a tear would roll down if there were one.

"Well, I guess it's all's well that ends well," Jessie said, giving Slater a private smile.

"Thanks for being so understanding," Dolores said to them. "The funny thing is, I managed to make a really good friend, anyway. And it didn't have anything to do with my master plan."

"There's just one thing I want to know," Kelly said. *"Who is Rupert?"*

Dolores flipped her red hair over her shoulder. "Zack's cousin, of course. Don't you guys know him?"

The gang all exchanged glances.

"Rupert?" Jessie said questioningly.

"I guess you haven't seen much of him since he travels so much," Dolores said. "Monte Carlo, Switzerland, you know. I just think it's great that Zack has a cousin from Studovia. I just love his accent. And it's so funny that the two of them look like twins!"

"That *is* funny," Kelly said, shooting Zack a nasty look.

Zack wanted to sink through the floor. It was clear that he had some major explaining to do. Somehow he knew that no matter *how* much he did, he still wouldn't get out of the doghouse with Kelly.

Well, at least there was still Dolores. Now that Rupert was moving back to Europe, Zack could move in. A little guilt from her false accusation could go a long way.

Dolores checked her watch. "Listen, you guys, I've got to run. Remember that new friend I was telling you about?" Her topaz eyes sparkled, and she grinned.

"Ah-ha," Lisa said. "Somehow I think that this is a *male* friend."

"Exactly," Dolores said. "And he's a dream. Gorgeous, handsome, and sweet."

"Whoa," Lisa said. "Who is this guy and why haven't I checked him out?"

"He's new here, too," Dolores confided. "His name is Cody Durant. I met him at the beach, and I told him I'd meet him there this afternoon. See you later."

Dolores ran out of the room happily. Kelly stared after her, openmouthed. Then she turned to Zack.

"This is all your fault!" she hissed. "And you'd better not write Dolores any letters for Cody, either."

"So tell us about Rupert, Zack," Slater said wickedly. "How come you didn't introduce us?"

"Yeah," Screech said. "I'd like to meet your cousin."

"There is no cousin, Screech," Lisa told him. "Zack made him up."

"And I think I know why," Slater said. "It's because Dolores thought you were a bum. Everybody knew she wanted a sophisticated guy. Pretty smart, Morris. Too bad you got caught."

Zack eyed Kelly uneasily. She didn't look angry anymore. As a matter of fact, she looked kind of sad. That made him feel worse than ever.

"I was just trying to make Dolores feel at home," he said. "I felt sorry for her. I was trying to bring her a taste of home. How could I know that home was really Gary, Indiana? It was just my way of unrolling the Bayside High welcome mat."

"Don't bother, Zack," Kelly said. Her voice sounded tight, as though she were fighting back tears. "We all know you were chasing Dolores. And to think I actually thought that you . . . To think that when I reread those letters, I actually wondered . . ."

Zack knew immediately what she meant. "I *did* mean those things, Kelly," he said desperately. "Every one of them."

"Give me a break," Kelly said flatly. "If you think I'm going to believe that, you're crazy. I'm

not that stupid, Zack! I mean, I might have been—
but not anymore. And never again."

Choking back a sob, Kelly rushed from the room.
Zack slowly sank down on the tarp.

"Well," Slater said philosophically, "you may
not be the prankster, but you're still a number
one jerk."

"You can say that again," Zack moaned.

"You're a number one jerk," Screech said help-
fully.

Zack sighed. "Thanks, Screech. I can always
count on you in a pinch."

"Hey, I'm not going to pinch you, too," Screech
protested. "There I draw the line."

▲   ▼   ▲

Later that night, Kelly sat in the deserted Max
all alone, nursing a hot-fudge sundae. Even extra
whipped cream hadn't made her feel any better,
though. In only one week, she'd found out her true
love, lost her true love, and almost found another
old love. She felt sad, but she also felt exhausted.

A jangling interrupted her thoughts, and she
looked up to see Rosina, the gypsy. "It's you!"
Kelly said.

Rosina nodded. "You look very unhappy, young
lady," she said in her thick accent. She was still

wearing sunglasses, even though the sun was down. Kelly guessed that she still had her eye infection.

Rosina slid into the booth with a jangling and clanging of necklaces. "Oh, Rosina," Kelly said with a sigh. "I was so happy after you told my fortune, and now I'm completely miserable."

"And vat ees meking you meeserable?" Rosina asked, adjusting the flowing scarf on her head.

"You told me who my true love was, and I lost him," Kelly said sorrowfully. "But now I'm wondering if I really loved him. And I'm not sure if Cody really loved me."

"Who ees thees Cody?" Rosina asked. "I did not see a Cody in your feet."

"But you said . . . Well, I´guess you didn't say, exactly," Kelly admitted. "I just assumed it was Cody."

"And zat was your first mistake," Rosina said. "I'm the fortune teller, sveetheart, not you."

Kelly leaned over the table. "Then can you tell me who my true love really is?"

Rosina shrugged, and the little bells on her necklace tinkled. "But of course. Ees easy."

"Who?" Kelly breathed. "And be specific. I don't want to mess up again."

"No problem. Eet ees Zack."

"Zack?" Kelly asked incredulously. "Zack Morris?"

Rosina nodded. "Exactly."

Kelly slowly fell back. "Wow," she said. "This is amazing. My true love *is* Zack."

Her business done, Rosina slid out of the booth. "I hope I have helped you, young lady."

Kelly nodded, her blue eyes shining. "Oh, absolutely. You've been superhelpful. I finally know what to do."

Rosina paused. "And what weel you do?"

"Well, now that I know Zack and I will end up together eventually, I can prepare," Kelly said. "You see, the teen years should be a time of experimentation and exploration. That's the only way I can learn how to be a good life partner. In the rain forest of life, why carry a defoliant?"

Rosina passed a faltering hand to her brow. "So vat you are saying ees—"

"That it's time to date like mad!" Kelly said enthusiastically.

Rosina keeled over in a dead faint. Kelly jumped up, then leaped over Rosina's inert body to get help. *Funny,* she thought as she raced to the kitchen. *Rosina is wearing running shoes just like Zack's. How about that—even gypsy fortune-tellers like to jog!*